Lying In Bed, Staring Into The Darkness, Caitlyn Remembered The Single Kiss She Had Shared With Rafaelo.

She moved restlessly, the cotton sheets cool and smooth against her hot, aching skin. The response the Spanish nobleman had aroused in her was intense, physical, consuming. If only he wouldn't be leaving once he got what he'd come for.

What he'd come for...

His share of Saxon's Folly.

Suddenly she felt chilled, and the darkness seemed to turn hostile.

Rafaelo would never be able to reconcile with the Saxons. There was too much bad blood between them. And she was trapped in the middle— between the family she adored, and the man she was coming to love....

Dear Reader,

Caitlyn Ross is a gutsy character who tugged at my heartstrings from the first moment I met her in *Mistaken Mistress,* the opening book in the THE SAXON BRIDES trilogy. Caitlyn yearns for love. And when Rafaelo sprang to life, I knew I had found the man for her.

Passionate. Sensual. Mediterranean. Rafaelo is a special kind of hero—he's a Spaniard. But to Caitlyn, there is the danger that he can destroy the family she loves so dearly.

Yet despite the many things that divide Rafaelo and Caitlyn—opposing loyalties, past traumas and vastly differing upbringings—both of them overwhelmingly love the rich traditions of making wine. To each of them, *terroir,* a French word describing a very special piece of dirt that is the birthplace of great wines, is *almost* as important as family.

Please share Rafaelo and Caitlyn in discovering the joy—and confusion—of love. And please visit www.tessaradley.com to find out more about upcoming SAXON BRIDES books.

Take care,

Tessa

SPANIARD'S SEDUCTION

TESSA RADLEY

Silhouette®

Desire

Published by Silhouette Books

America's Publisher of Contemporary Romance

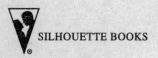

SILHOUETTE BOOKS

ISBN-13: 978-0-373-76907-0
ISBN-10:   0-373-76907-5

SPANIARD'S SEDUCTION

Books by Tessa Radley

Silhouette Desire

Black Widow Bride #1794
Rich Man's Revenge #1806
*The Kyriakos Virgin Bride #1822
*The Apollonides Mistress Scandal #1829
*The Desert Bride of Al Zayed #1835
Pride & a Pregnancy Secret #1849
†*Mistaken Mistress* #1901
†*Spaniard's Seduction* #1907

*Billionaire Heirs
†The Saxon Brides

TESSA RADLEY

loves traveling, reading and watching the world around her. As a teen, Tessa wanted to be an intrepid foreign correspondent. But after completing a Bachelor of Arts and marrying her sweetheart, she became fascinated by law and ended up studying further and practising as an attorney in a city practice.

A six-month break traveling through Australia with her family reawoke the yen to write. And life as a writer suits her perfectly; traveling and reading count as research, and as for analyzing the world…well, she can think "what if" all day long. When she's not reading, traveling or thinking about writing she's spending time with her husband, her two sons, or her zany and wonderful friends. You can contact Tessa through her Web site, www.tessaradley.com.

It's people who make places great to work in.

To the team at Jay Inc…thanks for the wonderful years!

One

Rafaelo, Marques de Las Carreras, was seething with hot Spanish rage. And when Rafaelo seethed, wise people gave him a wide berth until he cooled down to his normal impeccable courtesy.

Rafaelo told himself he had reason to be furious. He'd flown from Spain via London to Los Angeles and on to his final destination of Auckland, New Zealand. A security furore in Heathrow had caused a six-hour delay, resulting in a missed transatlantic connection to the United States.

There had been no first-class seats available on the flight he'd finally caught and the carrier had been packed as full as a tin of *sardinas*. He'd been wedged between a sweating overweight car dealership owner and a fraught-looking woman with a screaming baby. It had not improved his mood.

By the time Rafaelo landed in Auckland eighteen hours later than scheduled, it was to discover that his monogrammed Louis

Vuitton luggage had vanished, and to top it all, the Porsche reserved for him had been hired out when he'd failed to turn up earlier.

Not even flashing traveller's checks, his platinum bank card or large-denomination American dollars could commandeer him a vehicle. Sorry, no cars available. There was an international sporting event on in the area, explained one car-hire company after another.

The Marques de Las Carreras wasn't accustomed to apologies, certainly not from an indifferent middle-aged woman filing her nails—who didn't respond to either his most charming smile or, when that failed to get results, to his dangerously lowered tone.

It was unheard of for him to be treated like a *peon*—usually his name was enough to secure him the best. The best seats at the bullfight, the best table in the restaurant, the best-looking woman in the room. And to come back to his present situation, the best car for hire.

He blinked, told himself this couldn't be happening. Finally he managed to rent a vehicle—if the battered and dented yellow-and-black apparition plastered with neon-coloured *Make Waves* and *Shoot the Tube* stickers could be called that—from an operator most appropriately named Wreck Rentals. It had cost him plenty.

Not only had he been royally ripped off, but he also hadn't slept in two days and a night. Nor had he showered. His clothes were creased. He was driving an abomination.

Twenty minutes later, teeth gritting as the thing—he couldn't truthfully label it a vehicle—shuddered, Rafaelo slowed at a large hand-carved sign welcoming visitors to Saxon's Folly Winery, home of the Saxon family.

The lane into which he turned was lined with established trees. Farther along the lane, a modern winery complex appeared. Through the trees Rafaelo glimpsed a large stately residence.

The car rolled to a stop.

He stopped breathing. The house was exactly as his mother

had described it. Tall. White. Lacy wrought iron trimmed the balconies. The elegant triple-storey Victorian homestead was drenched in history.

Cold purpose settled in the pit of his stomach.

Letting out the breath he'd been holding, he edged forward and parked the abomination in the shade of a giant oak. It was then that he discovered that the hand brake didn't hold. To Rafaelo's immense displeasure, he had to climb through a triple-strand wire fence to find a suitably large rock to place under the back tire, and by this stage his hands were dusty and his immaculate suit had a smudge of mud down the front.

"Madre de Dios," he cursed with quiet ferocity, then set off to find Phillip Saxon. And his destiny.

Caitlyn Ross noticed the stranger the moment he arrived at the memorial service being held for Roland Saxon in the winery's courtyard. Behind her the vineyards stretched to the hills in the distance, to the hills that formed The Divide. But for once she didn't spare a glance at the vines.

Her attention was riveted on the stranger. It wasn't his height, the dark, overlong hair or his black eyes that caught her attention. With Heath and Joshua Saxon in the vicinity, there was no shortage of tall, dark, black-eyed men.

Rather, it was the fire that lit those black eyes and made them snap with energy, the way he stood holding himself with stiff formality at the back of the crowd that had gathered to remember Roland Saxon.

She had no idea who he could be. Or what his association to the Saxons was. And that was unusual. Having worked here since she left university, Caitlyn was part of the inner circle of the family. But this man was definitely a stranger.

Beside her, someone sniffed and pulled out a handkerchief. Phillip Saxon had finished his speech.

Remembering the occasion, Caitlyn forced her attention away from the mystery man. Alyssa Blake was speaking now, a short, moving address. Roland had been her brother. No one had known that he'd been adopted by the Saxons as a baby until very recently. Caitlyn knew it had to be a huge adjustment for Heath, Joshua and Megan, the Saxon siblings, who had believed that Roland was bonded to them by blood.

Her gaze sneaked back to the stranger. Even sandwiched between Jim and Taine, two of her cellar hands, he stood apart. She watched as he scanned the gathering, those snapping eyes assessing…making a judgement…then moving on to the next person.

Who was he?

Yet another journalist come to dig up dirt on the family? They didn't need that. Not now.

She examined the tall, suit-clad body. Despite the dusty patches on his suit, he didn't look like a journalist. He couldn't be paparazzi because there was no giveaway bulge of an over-sized camera lens anywhere to be seen. She supposed he could be a school—or university—friend of Roland.

Caitlyn slipped through the throng, murmuring apologies as she went. It took her only a minute to skirt the edges of the gathering. She paused beside Jim, who made way for her with a sideways smile. Caitlyn nodded in acknowledgement and edged into the space created beside the stranger.

Yes, he was tall all right. At least three inches taller than her own five feet eleven inches.

Softly she murmured, "We haven't met."

He raked her with those hellfire eyes. A bolt of sensation shot through her. An awareness that she hadn't felt in a long, long time.

"I am Rafaelo Carreras." His voice was mesmerizing, the accent deliciously foreign. Within Caitlyn, in a deep-down sealed-off place, warmth uncurled. She tamped down the unwelcome sensation. No hint of New Zealand in that voice.

Perhaps not a school friend after all.

Curious, and wanting to hear him speak again, she asked, "Did you know Roland?"

It was possible. As marketing director of Saxon's Folly Estate & Wines, Roland had travelled all over the world.

"No."

One word, abruptly spoken. And clearly he wasn't volunteering any further information. Again the suspicion that he might be a news journalist, carrion descending to feast on the family's sorrow, stirred. The Saxons had been through enough. All her protective urges aroused, Caitlyn said in a low, fierce voice, "Then what are you doing here?"

He inspected her. His narrowed gaze started at her shoes—the serviceable black leather pumps that she'd had for ten years and only wore for wine shows. He considered her unstockinged legs, pale from a longer-than-normal winter spent under worn jeans. His gaze lingered on the hemline of her skirt, an unfashionable length this season. But then, she never wore anything other than jeans and trousers, so what did it matter? Then he studied the jacket that she wore. It had cost her a fortune and she'd only bought it because Megan, whose sense of style was fabulous, had insisted. The peach-coloured linen did wonderful things for her Celtic skin and ginger-blond hair—she knew that because Megan had told her—but it probably wasn't suitable for today's sombre occasion.

Finally he lifted his eyes to her face. As his gaze met hers, the impact jarred through her. There was nothing in the black depths to suggest that he'd liked anything he'd seen. To the contrary, she could find only a disdain that made her flinch.

"You are a member of the Saxon family?" He raised a haughty brow.

"No, but—"

"Then why I am here does not concern you."

Caitlyn blinked. She was not used to such blatant rudeness. How to deal with him? Her gaze flickered to Pita, the security guard who patrolled the winery every night. Since an incident three weeks ago when a pair of youths had caused mischief down at the stables, security at Saxon's Folly had been stepped up. Pita was big and burly. He would have plenty of men here to help evict this man if need be.

She eyed the dark-haired stranger covertly. It would take quite a few men to restrain him. Under the dark suit his body appeared lean and his shoulders broad. The man was built like a fighter— an impression strengthened by the harsh features, the ridged nose and fiery eyes. He wouldn't back away from a fight.

She held his gaze. "Well, I am concerned."

"Don't be."

His mouth clamped into a hard line causing apprehension to weigh heavily in Caitlyn's stomach. Another quick glance showed that Pita was still within earshot. She wavered. Should she summon him…have the stranger escorted away?

Did the Saxons need the commotion? She glanced around the gathering. Alyssa was speaking in a breaking voice about how she'd grown to know Roland through the memories of his mother and his siblings—Joshua, Heath and Megan. No, commotion was the last thing the Saxons needed right now.

What if this man turned out to be a valuable business connection? And she'd tried to have him thrown out? Caitlyn shuddered just thinking about it. No, she'd leave him alone. For now.

A rustle and the soft murmurs of the crowd caught her attention. Alyssa had finished speaking and was stepping down from the paved stage, wiping her eyes. Joshua Saxon moved forward and put his arm around her, his head close to Alyssa's as he led her away. Joshua and Alyssa were engaged now. Despite the upheavals in the past month, they had managed to find each other…and love.

A pang of some unfamiliar emotion shot through Caitlyn. Not jealousy—she'd never felt anything vaguely romantic toward Joshua—but something a little like envy.

She wanted to find love.

She was tired of being Caitlyn Ross, chief winemaker at Saxon's Folly, top graduate of her year…the smart student that all her fellow students considered one of the boys.

She wanted what other people had.

Love. Togetherness. A life.

But she knew that her chances of that were scant. Not that she was complaining. There was nothing wrong with her life. She loved Saxon's Folly. There had been a time when she'd hoped she and Heath Saxon might…

But there was little chance of that now. And to be truthful Heath had never seen her as anything other than Good Ol' Caitlyn. Damn, she was practically one of the boys.

Although nothing about the bold inspection she just received made her feel remotely like one of the boys. She resisted the temptation to slide her gaze sideways to the stranger beside her. His inspection had been heavy with male arrogance, but there was no doubt that he'd been assessing her as a woman.

Even if he had found her wanting.

It had been so long since she'd drawn any male attention— these days she took care to avoid it. At last, against her will, resenting the effect he had on her, she gave in to temptation and peered sideways, to see what those never-still eyes were looking at now, and her stomach plummeted into her practical black shoes.

He was gone.

Rafaelo had found his target.

Silently, unwaveringly, he made his way in the direction of the tall man with the distinguished wings of grey at his temples.

Phillip Saxon.

He stopped behind the older man and waited for what was clearly a memorial ceremony to end. He'd wanted to savour this meeting. He'd called Saxon, spoken to his PA, and without listening to her protests that Saxon wasn't seeing people right now, had advised that he would be arriving to meet with the older man. He hadn't revealed why he wanted to see Saxon—only that he was the owner of a Spanish vineyard of some reputation. But he hadn't planned for this meeting to take place in public.

A movement behind him caught his eye. Rafaelo frowned impatiently as he watched the crowd part for the tall, slim strawberry blonde who had waylaid him minutes before.

He tightened his lips as she came closer. She was not beautiful—she lacked the self-awareness that beautiful women possessed. But she had something…

Then he met her startlingly pale blue eyes, read the determination in them.

He glanced dismissively away. She couldn't stop what he'd come all the way to New Zealand to achieve. Nor would he allow himself to be distracted.

The crowd was shifting. A tall, black-haired man stood at the edge of the courtyard beside a vine and a rosebush that the raw earth beneath revealed had recently been planted.

"These have been planted in the memory of my brother, Roland. May he live in our hearts forever," the black-haired man said.

All around Rafaelo women were reaching for handkerchiefs. But he barely heard the gut-wrenching sobs of sorrow. He only heard the words *my brother, Roland.* So Roland Saxon was dead. That would make the speaker either Joshua or Heath Saxon. An unfamiliar heavy heat coalesced in his chest.

He turned to gaze at Phillip Saxon and instantly the emotion became identifiable. *Rage.* Saxon moved forward, away from him. The ceremony had ended.

Now.

Rafaelo tapped him on the shoulder. *"Disculpe."*

The older man spun round.

There was a long silence as Rafaelo stared into Phillip's face. He examined the narrow nose. The dark hair that sprung back from a high forehead. He stared into the dark eyes—so like his own—and watched them widen.

"No." The denial burst from Saxon.

Another beat of time passed. Rafaelo waited, letting the other man put it all together.

"It can't be." Saxon was shaking his head.

"Phillip?" The strawberry blonde stood there. "Is everything okay?"

Rafaelo resented his focus being taken from Saxon. But he did a double take at the unfriendly suspicion in the pale eyes that clashed with his. A frisson of a wholly unfamiliar sensation prickled the back of his neck. He did a startled double take.

Get rid of her. As a young man he'd survived countless bullfights by listening to his senses. He heeded the warning now.

"We would like some privacy, please," he demanded, giving her the freezing glare that he usually reserved for the paparazzi.

Phillip looked horrified at his statement.

"Do you want me to go?" Her words were directed at Saxon, but she never took her eyes off him.

"No—stay."

Rafaelo reassessed. She must be more important than he'd initially thought. *Estupido!* He could kick himself for dismissing her as a nonentity. Narrowing his eyes, he scrutinised her. He knew she wasn't Megan Saxon—he'd met Megan once, briefly, at a wine show in France several years before. This woman was too tall and her colouring was all wrong. And she'd denied being part of the family earlier.

So who the devil was she? He examined her from head to toe,

ignoring her indrawn breath. She lacked the polish of the circle the Saxons moved in, lacked the salon-set hair, the designer-label clothes. That meant she had to be an employee, he decided. A presumptuous one.

"You want her to stay? On your head may it rest," Rafaelo addressed Saxon. "I didn't think you'd want this conversation to be public knowledge. At least not until we've had an opportunity to negotiate."

Saxon understood. His spine straightened and relief flashed in his eyes, coupled with contempt.

He thought he could buy off Rafaelo.

"Caitlyn, perhaps you should leave us."

Caitlyn? That would be Caitlyn Ross. Rafaelo did a double take. She didn't look anything like what he'd anticipated of the acclaimed Saxon's Folly winemaker. He'd thought she'd be older for starters. More sophisticated. This woman looked to be in her midtwenties, too young to have accomplished everything that his research had told him she had.

Caitlyn was shaking her head. "No way am I leaving you alone with him. What he—" she jabbed a slender finger in Rafaelo's direction "—said sounded like a threat." The pale eyes duelled with his. "I'm staying right here."

Brave, too. Foolishly so. "You should stay out of things that do not concern you," he told her, lowering his voice.

"So now you're threatening *me*." Colour flooded her translucent skin.

"Advising, not threatening. There is a difference," Rafaelo pointed out with gentle irony. "This is family business…." He drew the phrase out mockingly. "It has nothing to do with you." Then he turned his narrow-eyed attention back to Phillip Saxon.

"The family's business has everything to do with me," she said hotly.

"Caitlyn is like family," Phillip spoke at the same time.

The look she gave Saxon was filled with gratitude—and annoyed Rafaelo immensely. He pushed his hands into the pockets of his suit pants and glared at both of them.

Saxon swallowed convulsively and Rafaelo watched mercilessly as the man sought the words that might make Rafaelo go away.

He wouldn't find them.

For the first time since he'd learned the truth, Rafaelo felt his heart lighten. He started to enjoy himself. Saxon was in a tight spot and he wouldn't get out. And this woman, who looked as innocuous as milk and honey, was proving to be a challenge that he had not foreseen.

"Caitlyn, dear, where did you arrange with the caterers for the canapés to be served?" Kay Saxon sounded harried as she joined them.

As Caitlyn opened her mouth to answer Saxon's wife, Rafaelo stepped forward. "Introduce us," he commanded.

Phillip Saxon blanched. He gave his wife an agonised look, and then his eyes darted back to Rafaelo.

"I… Kay, this is—" He broke off.

Rafaelo waited in stony silence.

"I'm sorry," Phillip said at last, "I do not know your name."

Rafaelo smiled. It was not a nice smile. He was too angry for that. "My name is Rafaelo Carreras."

The wife gave him a polite smile and held out her hand. "How do you do, Mr. Carreras."

So she thought him a business associate. She had absolutely no idea. Rafaelo's smile widened and his anger sharpened. "Ah, a handshake is so English. And I know we will be getting to know each other extremely well." He stepped forward and brushed her cheeks with his in the European way. Over her shoulder he saw the horror…the despair…in Phillip Saxon's eyes. He had the look of a man tied to the railway tracks in the face of the rush of an oncoming express—his tortured expression revealed that he knew the crash was inevitable, that he could do nothing except wait for the approaching disaster.

Good, the man was afraid. Phillip Saxon had sensed that he, Rafaelo, could destroy his privileged world, everything he held dear.

Then a movement forced his attention to Caitlyn. Her hand was outstretched. "If you're going to get to know the Saxons well, then we'd better introduce ourselves, too. I'm—"

He ignored the proffered hand, and her introduction trailed away into silence. Placing his hands on her shoulders, he leaned forward. She smelled of wildflowers, soft and subtle.

"Encantado de conocerte." Very happy to meet you. His lips brushed one cheek, he heard her gasp. His head lifted. Deliberately he kissed her other cheek, no social brush, but a careful placing of his mouth against the pale, silken milk-and-honey skin. He paused for a moment before whispering in her ear, "The pleasure is all mine, Miss Ross."

She pulled back, a startled expression on her face, a touch of fear in her eyes. "You know my name?"

She was too modest. Of course he knew her name. Rising star. Winner, two years ago, of a silver medal at the World Wine Challenge. And last year she and Saxon had secured a coveted gold medal. His mouth curved. "You'd be surprised by how much I know."

He heard Phillip's indrawn breath.

The fear subsided and her eyes sparkled with anger. "Perhaps you don't know as much as you think, Mr. Carreras. It's *Ms.* Ross."

"Ah," he said softly, eyes narrowing at her attempt to hold him at a distance with icy formality. "I should've known." And he watched the fresh annoyance flare in those pale, clear eyes.

He preferred her anger to her fear. For a split second he wondered what she was afraid of—because she couldn't know why he was here. Then Saxon shifted and he moved his attention back to the man he'd come across the world to find.

"Caitlyn, Kay, perhaps it is better that I speak to Mr. Carreras alone." Saxon sounded anxious.

A frown pleated Kay's forehead. "But why should that be necessary?"

"There may be things that your husband hasn't told you, Mrs. Saxon." The address held a certain irony that only Rafaelo was aware of.

She waved a dismissive hand. "My husband tells me everything."

"Perhaps not." Rafaelo's mouth slashed upward.

"You're impertinent."

It was not Kay Saxon who spoke. Rafaelo turned his attention on the blonde. If anyone was impertinent, it was her. He was the Marques de Las Carreras. All his life the family name had commanded respect. Until now…

"Be careful," he murmured.

"Or what?" Caitlyn challenged. "What are you threatening to do? This is Saxon property, there is security—" She gestured toward a burly man in a dark uniform.

"Caitlyn." Phillip put a hand on her arm.

But with her protective instincts roused, she would not be stopped. "Call Pita. He can't just walk into Saxon's Folly and threaten you, Phillip."

Rafaelo stared at her. "I am not threatening anyone. I will not be evicted. But I am certain that that he—" Rafaelo couldn't bring himself to address the man directly "—would prefer to talk alone."

Phillip released her. "Caitlyn, perhaps he is right."

"I would like to hear what this man has to say, what he thinks you might not have told me." Kay Saxon dug her Ferragamo-clad heels into the ground. "Caitlyn is right—he is impertinent."

Anger ignited deep in Rafaelo's heart. All the inconveniences of the past two days flamed high, and the pain and rage he'd been keeping under tight control for the past months burst into a blinding conflagration.

He raised an arched, black eyebrow. "It is impertinent to travel all the way to New Zealand to meet my father?"

Phillip dropped his head forward into his hands and uttered a hoarse groan.

"Your father?" Caitlyn looked bewildered. "What does that have to do with—"

Rafaelo glared at her. "It has nothing to do with you—it is a family matter. But trust me, Phillip Saxon is my father."

Two

Trust him?

Never! Caitlyn drew a shaking breath but kept quiet. Lashing out at the arrogant Spaniard wouldn't help the fact that she'd exposed Kay to a dreadful revelation.

If she hadn't pushed him, challenged him, the outcome might have been very different…

"What did you say your name was?" Kay was asking Rafaelo, her face suddenly pale.

"Rafaelo Carreras."

Slowly Kay started to shake her head. "I don't know anyone by that name."

"He's lying," Caitlyn said fiercely, determined not to let Kay be upset. She had enough to contend with already.

"Kay—"

"Wait." Kay warded off Phillip's attempt to talk to her. "Carreras, it's Spanish, isn't it?"

Caitlyn didn't like the sudden gleam in Kay's eyes. Nor, it appeared, did Phillip.

"Kay, love, let's go. There are people waiting to pay their respects." Phillip curled an arm around his wife's shoulders, the skin stretched thin across his cheekbones.

But Kay didn't budge.

Rafaelo placed his hands on his hips, and thrust his shoulders forward. He looked ready for battle. "Madam, my full name is Rafaelo Lopez y Carreras."

"Lopez? There was a girl…a young woman…" Kay's brow pleated as her voice trailed away. "I think her name was Maria Lopez. In fact, I'm sure of it. She was researching her family… I seem to remember that her father, or perhaps an uncle, had died in the Napier earthquake. Yes, that's right. It's coming back to me. Her name *was* Maria."

"My mother's name is Maria," Rafaelo said in a flat voice, his eyes shooting daggers at Phillip.

Eyes widening, Kay put her hand over her mouth and, shrugging out from under his arm, turned to her husband. "Tell me this isn't true."

Caitlyn's stomach dropped like a stone at the expression in Kay's eyes. She clenched her hands into fists. Surely, Kay couldn't believe what Rafaelo claimed was true?

Phillip took a large white handkerchief from his pocket and, without unfolding it, rubbed it across his brow.

"You are not going to deny it, are you?" Kay's face had drawn into tight lines. She turned her attention back to Rafaelo, studying him with critical eyes. "How old are you?"

"Thirty-five."

Kay was not telling Rafaelo to get lost.

"That's the same age as Roland." Kay paused and sucked in an audible breath. "When were you born?"

Rafaelo told her.

Hurt flickered across Kay's face. "That makes you Phillip's eldest son…even if Roland our—my—first child hadn't died."

There was a world of reproach in the look that Kay gave Phillip.

Hurriedly he reached for her. "Kay, I'm sorry. I never—" He broke off, shamefaced.

"Never wanted me to know?"

Phillip didn't answer and Kay tugged her hand free and walked away. After a horrible silence, Phillip took off after her.

Finding that her hands were shaking, Caitlyn balled them against her mouth. God. It had all happened so fast…

And it appeared that Rafaelo wasn't lying.

A sideways glance revealed that Rafaelo's face held no expression. No glee. No gloating. So why had he done it? Why had he come all the way across the world and dropped this devastating bombshell on the Saxons?

He met her questioning gaze with a decided lack of expression and said, "So I am not a liar."

Then Rafaelo was walking away from her, too, his back ramrod-straight, his black head held at a proud, arrogant tilt. Caitlyn stared after him, her mouth hanging open. Finally she came to her senses.

"What were you hoping to achieve by staging that little scene?" She hurled the words like pebbles at the space between his shoulders.

He stopped, then turned.

Caitlyn glanced around. A little way off a couple stared curiously in their direction. Farther away groups stood around talking. "It's too public here for the conversation I have in mind. Come with me."

He didn't look like the kind of man who followed orders. She half expected him not to follow as she crossed the lane that led past the winery to the house and wound her way along the shoulder of the hill, down the northern slope planted with

Cabernet Franc vines. For once Caitlyn didn't notice the pale green of the leaves, or how the land opened up to meadows where wildflowers had started to bloom in deep drifts along the fence line. She was too mad.

His fault.

Normally, she was even-tempered, easy to get along with—she never lost her temper and rarely even told off any of her cellar hands. But Rafaelo Carreras had managed to get under her skin with his intransigence, with his hard-ass, unbending attitude. She glanced back, he was following. Good.

She quickened her pace.

Caitlyn took him to the stable block. As they entered the yard in front of the L-shaped block, several horses stuck their heads over the half doors, ears pricked with interest. The familiar warm smell of horses and hay calmed her a little. At the end of the row, one stall was closed top and bottom and Caitlyn could hear the animal inside battering the door with his hooves as he demanded to be let out.

That would be Lady Killer. Apart from him, there should be no interruptions. Certainly, there would be no danger of being overheard by guests who'd come to attend Roland's memorial service.

She swung around and glared at Rafaelo. "Do you have any idea what you interrupted?"

"I called the winery. I made an appointment."

Caitlyn raised her eyebrows. "I don't think so. Not for today. Not when Kay and Phillip are unveiling a memorial plaque for their son."

"No, no. The appointment was for yesterday." His hands raked his hair. "But I experienced some delays."

She scanned his appearance. Not even the wrinkles and specks of dust could hide the fact that the suit was unlike anything she'd seen before. It fitted like it had been handmade—even if it was looking a little shabby right now. "The security scare in London?" She nodded at his startled look. "I heard about it on the news. I'm sorry, but Phillip and Kay haven't been taking appointments for the last few days."

He looked a little abashed. "The woman who answered the phone said something but I wasn't listening."

So he wasn't lying. The frustration in his eyes was too real.

"You must've spoken to Amy, the winery's PA. Roland was her fiancé." Poor, poor Amy. She would almost certainly not have remembered to tell Phillip about any appointment. She was perilously close to a breakdown. "So I'm sorry, but Phillip probably didn't get the message." But that still didn't excuse Rafaelo's harsh behaviour. "Once you realised that a memorial ceremony was taking place, couldn't you have left?"

"So the memorial service is for Roland? The eldest son?"

His face wore a strange expression. Caitlyn gave up trying to decipher what it meant. "Yes, Roland died in a car accident, several weeks ago." The night of the annual Saxon's Folly masked ball. "A terrible tragedy."

"My condolences." He bowed his head. Briefly. Politely. Then, like a dog with a bone, continued, "I have travelled many miles, I came with a purpose—I'd made an appointment. I wasn't to know Saxon knew nothing of it. Nor do I have any intention of turning tail and leaving without fulfilling that purpose."

"That's it? That's all you can say?" Caitlyn stared at him in disbelief. "After that confrontation you just forced?"

"I had no intention of forcing a confrontation—it was you who provoked that."

He gave her a frown filled with dislike. Caitlyn opened her mouth, then shut it again. Oh, why hadn't she stayed out of it?

Yet she knew that would've been impossible. She'd taken one look at the tall, dark foreigner, heard the sardonic edge to his voice as he harangued Phillip and she'd leapt into the fray to protect her employer. Hell, Phillip was more than an employer. He was her sounding board…her mentor…a dear friend.

"You must understand that the Saxons are like family to me." It was true. "I could no more leave you to bully Phillip than I could walk away from a delinquent drowning a kitten."

"I am not a bully," he growled, blood rushing under his olive skin. "I am not a delinquent. I do not drown kittens. I am a man of honour, something that your employer is not. I would never leave a young woman pregnant and alone."

Suddenly aware of his height and the strength of him as he loomed over her, Caitlyn felt a whisper of fear and took a step back.

He followed, relentlessly closing the space she'd claimed. "I wanted to face my cowardly father with the fact that he has a son he has never cared to acknowledge—and a woman who he had abandoned without giving her any emotional or financial support."

Another step and the whitewashed wall of the stables pressed against her back; Caitlyn could feel the roughness of the plaster through the linen jacket. She swallowed nervously. "Maybe he didn't know—"

"He knew!" Rafaelo loomed over her, dark and menacing, and planted a balled fist on either side of her head. "My mother wrote to him when she first learned she was pregnant."

"Perhaps—" Her voice cracked as he bent forward. Up close the snapping eyes were full of anger, his mouth drawn into a hard line that highlighted the small white scar below his bottom lip. No sign showed of the good humour that the laugh lines around his eyes suggested.

She didn't know this man at all.

He was a stranger.

What had possessed her to seek out privacy far from everyone else? Caitlyn swallowed again, horribly conscious of how isolated they were here in the empty stable yard.

Bravely she found her voice. "Perhaps the letter went astray."

"My mother wrote to him again, she was desperate. Is it likely that *two* letters went astray? New Zealand is, after all, hardly Mars."

The turmoil in his eyes twisted Caitlyn's insides into a knot and her anxiety about her own safety subsided. She fell silent. It *did* sound bad. But she couldn't believe Phillip would act so callously. Despite Rafaelo's accusations, she knew Phillip *was* a man of honour, a decent man, respected throughout the region for his business acumen and the fund-raising he did for charity.

She *had* to make Rafaelo understand that.

But before she could try to convince him, he pushed his hands away from the wall. The suffocating space between them widened, and Caitlyn sucked in a breath of relief.

"My mother even contacted him by telephone. Phillip Saxon made it clear that he wasn't interested in the child he had fathered, told my mother that he wouldn't be leaving his wife." There was a corrosive bitterness beneath that exotic accent.

Caitlyn glimpsed pain and suppressed rage in his expressive eyes. Unbidden, her hand came up, driven by an urge to rest it on his shoulder, to comfort him. Then the memory of his head bending over hers—of the suffocating closeness of a moment ago—returned and a sharp sliver of the poisonous fear pierced her. Hastily she dropped her hand to her side.

"There must have been some mistake," she whispered at last, thinking the response that he roused in her was definitely a mistake. She didn't want, or need, this.

"It was no mistake. Phillip Saxon abandoned her."

The edge in his voice took her mind off her body's incomprehensible reaction and made her think about what it must have been like for his mother to find herself alone and pregnant. Three decades ago it would have been worse; society had been much less accepting.

Yet Caitlyn couldn't help the wave of sympathy for Kay that

flooded her. Poor Kay! How humiliating this must be. How horrible to discover her husband's betrayal of their marriage vows at a time when she was struggling to come to terms with grief over the loss of her son.

In front of her Rafaelo shifted, his eyes unseeing, focused on an inner hell.

The last lingering vestige of apprehension left her. Caitlyn stepped away from the wall. "You're not the only one who has suffered." Surely Rafaelo would see that he had more in common with his father than he believed? "Phillip lost a son recently. Can't you find it in yourself to show him pity?"

"I'm well aware that I am not the only person to suffer bereavement." From this close her eyes were level with his mouth. His mouth…

Quickly she glanced up, only to find Rafaelo looking down his haughty nose at her. At once Caitlyn realised that he'd misunderstood her.

"I meant both of you are grieving. Perhaps you can offer comfort—"

"I have no intention of offering him anything," Rafaelo growled. "I owe him nothing. *Nada.*"

Caitlyn's cheeks grew hot at his stubborn intransigence. "He's your father, and he's just lost a son. Why don't y—"

The black eyebrows jerked together. Something violent flashed in the depths of his stormy eyes. "Phillip Saxon is *not* my real father. My father is dead. My father taught me to ride, to fish, to swim—and about wine. And that man is not Saxon."

"I'm sorry," she muttered in a subdued tone, not knowing what else to say.

He sighed then, a harsh, grating sound. "On his deathbed, the man who all my life I'd believed to be my father, informed me that he and my mother had lied to me, that I was not his son."

He'd felt betrayed. The sympathy Caitlyn felt for him grew.

It had been wrong of his mother to keep the truth from him. But what choice would Maria have had? She'd probably wanted to forget Phillip existed. Now Rafaelo had arrived at Saxon's Folly, betrayed, grieving…angry at the world.

It was an explosive situation. "Kay doesn't deserve—"

"I concede that my timing is unfortunate." The dark eyes lost a little of their angry fire. "But it was not my intention to deliberately set out to cause Kay Saxon pain."

"Only Phillip," she retorted, and watched his head jerk back. "You want to hurt him. *Why?* Because he rejected you when you were a child? Or because you're scared that he won't accept you now?"

A range of emotions flickered across his face, receding one by one, until only irritation remained. "I am not a child. I am a realist. I don't even know this man who fathered me—"

"But you want to get to know him?"

"No! I don't need to know him. I dislike him. I have no respect for hi—"

"So you want to wound him, don't you?" Caitlyn could feel herself getting hot and bothered as annoyance spread through her. "What do you plan to do to make up for the hurt he caused you?"

"It's not about me. I want the bastard to pay for what he did to my mother." The words burst from him in a torrent.

The silence that fell between them was deafening, broken only by the scrape of an iron shoe as a horse shifted.

Rafaelo looked astonished.

There was another emotion, too. Bewilderment? Confusion? Irritation? It passed too quickly for Caitlyn to read. Either way, it showed there was a chink in that impenetrable armour.

Before she could respond, her cell phone rang. "Where are you?" Megan demanded. "We need you."

Oh, damn. She was supposed to be helping with the reception.

"Be there shortly." Caitlyn hit the button to end the call.

Meeting his gaze, she said, "I have to go—and so should you. I think you've caused enough disruption today."

His eyes flashed. "I have every right—"

"Not today," Caitlyn said with certainty. "You need to calm down before you speak to your father." She tensed, waiting for him to rail at her for calling Phillip that. But to her surprise he didn't interrupt, so she continued, "Give the Saxons a chance to mourn, to remember Roland with dignity."

His eyes narrowed until all she could see were slits of onyx. "Tomorrow."

Caitlyn started to thank him. The compromise could not have been easy, but he steamrolled over her. "In the evening I am flying back to Spain. I do not have time to—how do you say?—twiddle my fingers."

"Twiddle your thumbs." She started to smile, refusing to let his disgruntlement spoil her pleasure in his concession. "It will be for only one night."

Rafaelo stared at her. Caitlyn shifted uncomfortably.

"You will have dinner with me tonight? At my hotel?"

Suddenly his eyes held a lazy warmth that turned Caitlyn's knees to liquid. The sensation was disturbing…and extremely unwelcome.

"No, I will not have dinner with you." She couldn't. Dared not. Not even to try and talk him out of the hatred he held toward the Saxons. "But may I suggest—"

"You are about to order me around again, *no?*"

She drew a deep breath. "No. Not order. Make a suggestion that will benefit both you and Phillip—and your relationship in the future."

"I have told you, I have no relationship with him." He was all disdain again, looking down that arrogant nose, the glimmer of interest that had warmed his eyes a moment ago well and truly doused.

The Spanish grandee, Caitlyn thought with a brief pang of regret at the loss of his more approachable manner. Then she said, "I think you do want a relationship with your father, otherwise why else did you come all this way?"

"Because—" He checked himself. "This is none of your concern."

Caitlyn suppressed the urge to roll her eyes skyward. "Oh, yes, because I'm not family, right?"

He stared at her unblinkingly, until an uncomfortable prickle started beneath the loose hair at her nape and shivered down her spine.

Hastily Caitlyn said, "I suggest that you spend the evening planning how best to cement the relationship with your father. I also think you should call tomorrow and let Phillip know that you're coming and give him some idea what you wish to see him about."

The edge of his lips curled up. The smile—if it could be called that—was full of male superiority and mockery. And it set her teeth on edge. It was a smile that made it clear that he would not take advice. Not from her. Not from anyone. Rafaelo Carreras was his own man and he would do what the hell he wanted.

Finally his lips moved. "It is not my way to let the opposition prepare."

Damn, but he was annoying with his formal diction, his immaculately tailored suit, and his give-not-one-inch manner…and that beautiful mouth that said such hateful, intransigent things.

"He's your father…not the opposition." Caitlyn heard her voice rising.

His face darkened and his lips parted.

She struggled for calm. "Okay, okay. You don't need to say it."

"Say what?"

"That he's not your father."

Rafaelo's mouth snapped shut, but his expression remained black as thunder. As she watched that very same mouth compressed into the hard line she was starting to recognise. Then he said, "Phillip Saxon has done nothing to earn the title of father. Right now he is my enemy."

Caitlyn tore her gaze from that riveting mouth and met the pair of black, smouldering eyes, where she read his implacable hatred for his father. And unexpectedly her heart ached for Rafaelo— and the Saxons.

After the disturbance he'd caused, Caitlyn was determined to escort Rafaelo politely off the estate herself even if the delay meant that she'd have to contend with Megan's wrath. She wanted no further chance encounters between Rafaelo and the Saxons. At least, not until this day was over.

But as she marched him back along the lane that led to the winery complex, Heath's voice broke in from behind them, "Caitlyn, do you know what happened to Mother? She's crying."

"Uh…" Caitlyn's heart sank and she suppressed the urge to utter a short, sharp curse. Making her way to the verge of the lane to get out of the path of an approaching car, she said, "Kay's crying?"

Kay hadn't cried since Roland had died. Her unnatural stoicism had caused the entire family much concern. But given today's emotionally charged occasion, it was hardly surprising that she'd broken down. Beside her Rafaelo paused, too. Caitlyn was aware of his body quivering with tension as he slowly turned to face Heath Saxon.

"I regret I said something that upset your mother." Rafaelo stood his ground, lean and dangerous as a jungle cat. "But that was never my intention."

Caitlyn looked from one man to the other—half brother to half brother. Now that she knew the truth she could see the similarities. Heath was younger, of course. But the dark eyes, the slope of their angular cheekbones, the determined set of the jaw branded them blood kin. Would Heath recognise it?

"What exactly did he say?"

Heath spoke directly to Caitlyn. He didn't even deign to look at the Spaniard. Misery sliced through Caitlyn as she recognised the icy set to Heath's features. She sensed the whole unfortunate situation was about to escalate to the next level.

And she had been the catalyst.

Before she could answer, Rafaelo cut in, "I am here, you may address me. I have a name. It is Rafaelo Carreras."

Heath gave him a brief, insultingly dismissive look. "Did you say something?"

Caitlyn tensed.

But Rafaelo didn't rise to the bait. "My name is Rafaelo Carreras—"

"I don't particularly care what your name is," Heath interrupted. "I want to know what you said to upset my mother."

Enough was enough. That had been more than rude; it had been downright incendiary. Caitlyn stepped between the two men.

"Heath—" She broke off and rested her hand on his arm, dearly familiar, and tried not to tremble.

It was painful to see Heath and Rafaelo bristling at each other like this. Profiles so similar, so classic, like two sides of an ancient coin.

"Heath, Caitlyn, Megan sent me to find you both. Aren't you coming to join our guests for coffee?" Joshua Saxon was crossing the cobbled lane toward them.

"First I want to hear what he—" Heath gestured to Rafaelo with a contemptuous flick of his head "—said to make Mother cry."

Joshua's eyebrows jerked up. "Mother is crying?"

"Yes, and he's responsible."

Caitlyn felt terrible. She'd caused this. If she'd left well enough alone, Rafaelo would have confronted Phillip alone—without her and Kay present—and there would've been a whole different outcome.

"Heath," she said. "It isn't his fault Kay is crying. It's m—"

"He might not have intended it." Heath shoved his shoulders forward. "But whatever he said still upset her." Heath ploughed forward, thrusting Caitlyn aside with one hand. She stumbled against the kerb stones. Heath made a grab for her, apologising profusely as she regained her footing.

Rafaelo moved like lightning, his jaw clenched tight. "Be careful," he snarled at Heath. To Caitlyn he said, "Are you okay?"

She gave him a small smile. "I'm fine. Just clumsy." The stumble had been worth it. It had checked Heath's aggressive rush at Rafaelo.

Except Rafaelo was staring at where Heath's hand rested on her arm. Discomforted, feeling as though she'd been caught doing something wrong, Caitlyn pulled free.

Heath raked his fingers through his hair. "You still haven't told me what you said to my mother." There was aggression in every line of Heath's lean, loose-limbed body. Caitlyn knew that stance. Even in university days, Heath-the-hellraiser had never backed away from a brawl, often throwing the first punch.

It would be terrible if he hit Rafaelo.

And for once, Caitlyn wasn't sure that Heath would win. Rafaelo looked tough and mean, his eyes narrowed, the small scar beneath his mouth pale against his dark skin. *A fighter.* An accomplished one, she suspected.

That thought was disturbingly disloyal.

Then Rafaelo's shoulders squared. "I came here today because six months ago I learned something has been kept secret from me all my life. I learned that the man I believed is my father never was, that a man who lives across the world is."

Caitlyn felt a little of the tension seep out of her. Rafaelo was making every attempt to stay calm and measured in the face of Heath's animosity. Perhaps the situation could still be saved.

"What does that have to do with—"

"You're Heath? Correct?" asked Rafaelo.

"Why are you asking?" demanded Heath.

Rafaelo shifted his attention to the taller of the two Saxons. "Then you must be Joshua."

Joshua nodded, his eyes hooded.

"I am Rafaelo—" he held up a peremptory hand as Heath started to interrupt "—and I am your half brother."

Heath sucked in his breath, an audible sound. "I don't think so. I think you're a scammer!"

"Heath!" Caitlyn's hands went to her mouth.

"This is not a scam." Rafaelo's hand dropped and curled into a fist at his side. "You think this is easy for me?"

"You expect us to believe that you found out six months ago? And it took you until now to act on this laughable claim?" Heath sneered. "Why wait so long?"

"I had responsibilities. I had a man to bury—the man I believed to be my father," Rafaelo said with what Caitlyn considered great restraint. "Afterward there was my mother to comfort and legalities to tend. I came as soon as my obligations allowed."

With Rafaelo standing to one side, his fisted hands the only evidence that he wasn't quite as relaxed as the curl of his lips would have them all believe, the air grew thick with menace. Caitlyn held her breath. Heath and Joshua stood shoulder to shoulder, brother beside brother, staring him down.

Caitlyn had seen that pose before. She shuddered. It wouldn't take much for the frozen tableau to ignite into a brawl.

Determined to prevent that at all costs, she stepped forward to stand beside Rafaelo and, without thinking, placed a hand on his arm. "Rafaelo is about to leave."

He turned his head. "I am?"

There was a sardonic light in his eyes.

She tightened her grip on his arm. With a sudden sense of

shock she felt the texture of the fine wool of his dark suit give under her fingertips, felt the hardness of flesh and muscle beneath. It scorched her.

"Yes, you are. I was walking you to your car," she said with quiet determination, even as her heart began to race, and the terrifying fear that she worked so hard to avoid bolted through her bloodstream.

"That's our Cait!" Heath said loudly. "Mate, you better do what she says if you know what's best for you."

Rafaelo went rigid under her hold. "I am not a milksop." He gave Heath an insulting head-to-toe-and-back-again look. "I do not let a woman placate the enemy on my behalf. I do what I want—not what a woman dictates." When his eyes met Caitlyn's appalled gaze, his features curdled with contempt. "So you fight his battles all the time?"

Instantly the thrill of apprehension that touching him roused and her irritation at his overt chauvinism were superseded by horrified concern. Not for him—if the Spanish grandee had his features rearranged by Heath it would serve him right. The concern was all reserved for Heath…for the Saxons. Kay would hate to learn that her sons had gotten into a brawl on this day because she'd cried.

Was Rafaelo stupid? Did he not realise what he was provoking? Or did he want a fight for reasons of incomprehensible masculine pride?

That notion caused her to worry even more. But there would be no fight. Not if she could help it.

"Sometimes the little woman knows best," Caitlyn cooed up at Rafaelo, fluttering her lashes, and moving squarely in front of him, daringly brushing his lapels free of imaginary fluff. Anything to stop Heath swinging the punch that she suspected was pending. But the tension in the lean body so close to hers, the sudden bulge in the chest muscles under her fingers, made her wish she hadn't been so reckless.

Heath watched and laughed uproariously. "Our kitten is now Cait-the-seductress. Priceless."

That hurt.

She blinked back the sudden prick of tears and, feeling totally ridiculous, she yanked her hands away from Rafaelo.

Furiously angry with Heath for highlighting how unwomanly she was, with Rafaelo for starting this whole debacle just by being there, and with Joshua for doing nothing to stop it, Caitlyn swung away, turning her back on all three of them.

"Fine," she said in a voice that indicated the situation was anything but okay. She pushed an annoying strand of hair out of her face, wishing it was back in its customary ponytail. And wishing that she could kick off the uncomfortable shoes and skirt and unfamiliar jacket. Above all, wishing she was a million miles from this maddening trio. "Do it your way. I'll just leave you all to bash each other's brains out. See if I care."

"Slowly, *querida.*" Rafaelo caught her arm.

His hold was firm, possessive. His fingers were square and tanned against the apricot hue of her jacket. No rings. But the knuckles were ridged. Yes, a fighter.

Shockingly, her arm started to tingle alarmingly under the warmth of his touch. Caitlyn lifted her gaze and gave him a fulminating glare. There was speculation in his expression—and something else. He glanced at Heath and back to her. He released her arm, and his gaze became calculating.

And that was when she knew that he'd seen what no one else had. The miserable remains of her hopeless infatuation for Heath.

Horror swept her. He wouldn't say anything, would he?

Then she realised that of course he would. Why shouldn't he? The damn man didn't like her one little bit. She'd been a thorn in his side since the moment he'd arrived. Why shouldn't he humiliate her?

But instead of adding to her humiliation, she heard him say,

"Caitlyn will walk with me. I am leaving. But be warned, I will be back."

Relief flooded her as he wheeled away from Joshua and Heath. But Caitlyn wasn't sure whether it was because the fist-fight had been forestalled...or because one of her heart's inner-most secrets had been saved. Either way, she couldn't help feeling a surge of gratitude toward Rafaelo as she trotted off in his wake.

Three

A lanky youth with a baseball cap jammed down on his head was standing with his back to the door when Rafaelo walked into the reception area of the winery the next morning.

"Buenos días," he said, "I'm looking for Phillip Saxon."

The youth turned and Rafaelo found himself staring into a pair of very familiar pale blue eyes. No youth this. Those unique eyes could only belong to one person…

Caitlyn Ross.

He did a rapid inspection to see how he could have made such an unforgivable mistake. The jeans she wore were faded and baggy, stained with the juice of grapes. The oversized navy-and-white striped T-shirt bore a sports team's logo and swamped her slender body. The baseball cap pulled low over her forehead hid the fine, beautiful copper-blond hair. Every trace of the feminine creature he'd met yesterday had vanished.

Except for the eyes.

Those hadn't changed. They met his directly, challenging him, stirring a primal need. The slow pounding of his heart under the force of her gaze ensured that he paid careful attention to everything about her.

"Did you call to let Phillip know you were coming?"

The awakening attraction withered. "Are you always so—" he searched for the word he wanted "—bossy?"

Irritation flashed in her eyes. She edged toward a stone archway. "I'm not bossy. I just don't want you causing trouble with the Saxons."

¡Vale! Okay, she'd made her feelings clear enough. Rafaelo followed her through the arch into the winery. Immediately the familiar smell of French oak surrounded him. Two rows of vats lined the long, dimly lit room where they stood. Another step forward brought a newer fragrance. The feminine fragrance of wildflowers. Caitlyn's fragrance.

Subtle. Evocative. Unexpectedly fragile.

Rafaelo drew a deep breath. "So you've decided that I'm the big bad wolf coming to eat your lambs?"

She shook her head. "I'd hardly describe Phillip or his sons as lambs."

Tipping his head to one side, Rafaelo said, "Perhaps they are the wolves...and I am the lamb?"

"Cute!" She beamed at him. It broke up the serious intensity of her face and revealed a dimple on the left side of her mouth and gave her expression a mischievous cast. "Definitely not. You're a wolf—pretending to be in lamb's clothing."

Desire jolted through him. But he wanted to laugh, too. The dimness of the winery seemed to grow brighter. The unrelenting heaviness that had consumed Rafaelo ever since he'd first learned he wasn't fathered by the man he'd always called *Papa* but by some not-so-perfect stranger who'd never wanted anything to do with him—or his sweet mother—started to lift.

"I am a Lopez on my mother's side—so maybe I am part wolf. You'd better take care and treat me with *mucho* respect." He gave her a lazy grin, showing his teeth, his heart lightening still further as her smile broke into peals of unrestrained laughter.

"Lopez? Oh, of course, lupis. Yes, you'd have to be a wolf."

Her gaze dropped to his mouth, and the fresh wave of desire that crashed through him shook Rafaelo to the core.

"My, my, what sharp teeth you have," she mocked gently.

"Is that an invitation for the wolf to bite?" He leaned toward her, drawn by the irrepressible sparkle in her eyes. The scent of wildflowers intensified. He wanted to yank her into his arms. Kiss her until she was breathless. "To hunt?"

She flushed, a flood of scarlet across the pale skin and drew quickly away, her smile fading.

"No…no."

The sudden panicked look she gave him made Rafaelo frown.

Before he could ask her what he'd done to bring that blind fear to her eyes, she shuffled away. "Uh, I have to go. You'll find Phillip in his office. Go out that door, past the stainless steel vats. Turn right and head down the corridor to the office at the end."

And then she was hurrying away without offering to show him the way into his father's lair. Rafaelo stared after her tall, slim body with consternation. What had happened? One moment she'd been laughing, teasing him…there'd been a bubble of suppressed excitement surrounding them…and then she'd run.

What had scared her? Him? *Dios,* he didn't pose any danger— at least, not to her.

Still trapped in a tizzy over the amused interest she'd glimpsed in Rafaelo's eyes and the shameful surge of desire that had been so quickly followed by fear, Caitlyn crossed the forecourt outside the brick structure that housed two immense stainless steel vats.

As she approached the tasting shed, a streak of silver flashed past her peripheral vision.

Heath.

She paused. For so long she'd been attuned to his every move. A glimpse of his silver Lamborghini usually stirred secret yearnings. Impossible yearnings. But today she merely frowned. With Rafaelo here, Heath's presence would only lead to more tension.

Heath seldom appeared during working hours. It was no secret that he and Phillip had differences of opinion—differences that had been significant enough for Heath to walk out of his job as winemaker at Saxon's Folly three years ago.

She lifted a hand and waved.

Heath waved back. Slowly Caitlyn made her way over to where he'd pulled the car in beside Rafaelo's beaten-up rental. Heath was already clambering out of the low-slung car under the angled doors.

Propping her hip against the battered vehicle, she folded her arms and asked, "What are you doing here?"

"Dad called. He wants me here for a meeting."

"Phillip called you?" She raised her eyebrows in surprise. Phillip and his youngest son usually did little but argue—each convinced that their own opinion was the only one that could be right.

"Yep. Before you start thinking reconciliation, he called Joshua, too. So your job is safe, kitten," Heath teased, ruffling the top of her head.

She ducked her head away and pulled off the baseball cap. "I'm not worried about you wanting my job. You put me up for it, remember?"

He tugged her ponytail. "Course I remember, rat's tail."

Instead of the hopeless longing that usually filled her at his joking, brotherly manner, Caitlyn felt only annoyance. And irritation with herself for wasting so much time on a man who never looked past the fact that she'd been a first-year student when he'd been studying for his doctorate. Then she'd been one of the few girls in a department dominated by guys and had chosen to become one of them—rather than the trophy that they bickered over, a path that would have put her truly on the outside.

She couldn't help thinking of the way that Rafaelo had looked at her in the winery earlier. His scrutiny had made her wish she hadn't been wearing scuffed sneakers and stained jeans.

That was until they'd started the talk about wolves and hunting, before she'd chickened out and hightailed it away as fast as her legs could carry her. Predatory males scared her spitless.

She shoved Rafaelo out of her thoughts and concentrated on Heath. "So Joshua is coming, too?"

"Yeah, apparently there's someone that Dad wants us to meet."

Rafaelo.

It had to be.

Phillip couldn't know that Joshua and Heath had already met Rafaelo yesterday…and almost come to blows.

Or maybe he did. "Uh…Heath…did you say anything to your parents about meeting Rafaelo yesterday?"

"Rafaelo?" Heath's cell phone started to ring and he dug into the pocket of his jeans to retrieve it.

"The Spaniard," she clarified, as the ringing grew louder.

"I remember exactly who Rafaelo is. I can't see why I should be bothering to discuss his spurious claim with Father."

Caitlyn waited as Heath answered his call, resting the phone in the angle between his shoulder and jaw.

"I'm here, Dad." He winked at Caitlyn. "What's the hurry?" He listened for a moment and all humour left his face, he started to frown. "Be there in two minutes."

His expression filled Caitlyn with dread. "What's the matter?"

"Sounds like Dad's got a bit of a problem."

"Problem?"

"Six foot–plus of pure bastard by the sounds of it. But not for much longer."

Heath tore across the drive, Caitlyn hard on his heels.

She thought of Rafaelo, his reluctance to call Phillip by his given name…or to acknowledge him as "my father." She thought of the isolation he must be experiencing among the tight-knit Saxon clan. She thought of Rafaelo standing toe-to-toe with Heath yesterday. She thought of his fury about Phillip's treatment of his mother.

Her heart sank. A fight was brewing. "Wait, I'm coming, too."

Caitlyn rushed into Phillip's office hard on Heath's heels. The office—if it could be called that—had windows with old-fashioned wide wooden sills that overlooked the vineyards, an antique desk clear of everything except a blotter and a gold pen in a marble holder, and a conference table with four chairs arranged around it. Three of the chairs were currently occupied by Phillip, Joshua and Rafaelo. The tension in the room was palpable.

"So this is about him?" Heath gestured with a thumb toward Rafaelo and took the last seat.

"Yes." Phillip did not elaborate.

Caitlyn hovered, feeling a little out of place—she was after all not family—then Rafaelo rose to his feet.

"Caitlyn…" he gave her name an exotic resonance "…take my chair."

"No, no, I'm fine."

"I insist." He stepped away from the table and perched himself on the windowsill.

"Sit down, Caitlyn."

She gave Phillip a quick smile. "Thanks."

Phillip didn't smile back. There were shadows of strain around his eyes, and a grim set to his mouth. He looked like he hadn't slept a wink last night.

Once seated, Caitlyn—and the Saxons—had to look up to Rafaelo where he sat, turning their heads at an uncomfortable angle. With the light behind him, it was impossible to read his expression. She wondered if Rafaelo had been aware of these advantages when he chose the spot by the window that put him outside the family circle.

Except the family circle was incomplete. At least two members were missing. "Where's Megan?" she asked.

"On her way," replied Josh.

"And Mother?" This time it was Heath who asked the question that Caitlyn had dared not voice.

Phillip hesitated. "She's working on a press release with Alyssa. She thought it better that she wasn't here. Alyssa excused herself, she says she needs to get the release off."

"But Mother always attends any family meeting." The words burst from Heath.

"Not this one apparently." Phillip looked pained.

Megan came through the door like a whirlwind. "Sorry, I was with Mum and Alyssa." She sounded out of breath, as though she'd been running.

"Here, have my seat," Caitlyn leapt up, increasingly conscious that while she was part of the inner decision-making team of Saxon's Folly, Rafaelo was right, this was not her business. This was family stuff. As much as she viewed the Saxons as extended family, she probably shouldn't even be here.

"Sit," Megan insisted. "I'll pull up Dad's desk chair." Heath rose and helped her bring it over. They all shuffled around to make space for her.

"Now what's this about?" Megan demanded.

Caitlyn squinted toward Rafaelo, interested to see how he was going to bridge the gap with his father…his siblings…to start to build the relationship that, despite his denials, she was convinced he'd come across the world to build.

"I want my share of Saxon's Folly." Rafaelo spoke from the window.

Caitlyn stared at Rafaelo in disbelief.

"*Your* share?" Heath was on his feet.

"Sit down, Heath," Phillip ordered.

Heath sank back, dark colour rising beneath his tan. He gave Rafaelo an unfriendly glare.

"Yes, my share." Rafaelo's voice was very smooth, his Spanish accent very evident. But Caitlyn noticed that sparks leapt from his eyes. He wasn't as calm as he appeared. "The birthright I was robbed of when he—" Rafaelo pointed at Phillip "—refused to acknowledge my mother's pregnancy."

"We've only got your word that my father is yours." Heath was the first to retort.

Rafaelo looked at him as though he'd crawled out of a muddy pond. "Even your mother acknowledges that my mother once lived in the area. Even she recognised the probability that—"

"*Probability?*" Heath mocked.

Joshua looked from one to the other. "Heath—"

"What?" Heath swung round. "He's scamming us—"

Joshua rested a steadying arm on his brother's forearm. "I wouldn't be so sure. Looking at the two of you is like looking into a slightly warped mirror. The resemblance is there, even though it's a little off."

Heath did a double take, then his gaze narrowed. "You're saying he's Dad's son?"

"I am! He—" Rafaelo nodded in Phillip's direction "—can confirm it."

"Sit." Joshua tugged Heath's arm. Once Heath had settled down, he added, "It's a definite possibility. He looks like us. His heritage is stamped all over his features. Given that, I don't think there's any point going down the prove-your-paternity road now. Although I'm sure Father will have the necessary DNA tests done." Joshua cast his father a glance.

"So what does that mean?" Megan asked.

"It means we have a problem. Rafaelo feels entitled to a share in Saxon's Folly. How are we going to solve this?" Joshua directed the last at Rafaelo.

"I want what I am owed."

The dark fire in Rafaelo's eyes that had so appealed to Caitlyn had subsided, leaving an empty void of black. No emotion. No anger. No hatred. Nothing that she could understand.

"What about your mother's responsibility in all this? Even what—thirty-something years ago?—women knew the risks of unprotected sex. It was hardly the dark ages." Megan shrugged. "I feel sympathy for your mother's plight, but she was foolish enough to mess around with a married man."

"She didn't know he was married." Rafaelo didn't raise his voice, but suddenly there was a sense of danger, a very real threat in the room. "He lied to her."

All the Saxon siblings looked to their father.

"Is that true?" It was Megan who asked the damning question that was in everyone's eyes.

"I don't remember—"

"Don't compound your lie with another." There was contempt in Rafaelo's voice.

Phillip dropped his head in his hands. "Okay, it's true. But later she knew I was married…and she didn't break it off."

"She loved you." Rafaelo's tone was thick with contempt. "She thought you were going to leave your wife and marry her."

Phillip's head reared back. "I *never* promised her that."

The Spaniard shook his head in disgust. "Tell them how young she was."

Phillip shook his head. "I don't remember."

The look Rafaelo gave him was loaded with disbelief. "She was eighteen. *Eighteen.* Little more than a child. And you took advantage of her inexperience."

"What about Mother?" Megan nailed him. "Did she know of this affair?"

Phillip shook his head. "Not until yesterday. After Maria left she never returned."

"But she tried to contact you." Rafaelo's mouth curled. "She came to New Zealand to visit the grave of her great-uncle Fernando, a monk who'd come from a Spanish monastery to follow his faith in Hawkes Bay. He'd died tragically in the earthquake of nineteen thirty-one. My mother was given the journals that he'd kept by a local historical society. She made the mistake of showing them to her lover—" he glared at Phillip "—who stole the methods Fernando had perfected."

Journals? Caitlyn's stomach tightened.

Phillip bent his head and stared blankly at the table in front of him. Then he murmured, "I do not have any such journals in my possession."

Misgivings filled Caitlyn. She was acquainted with the journals that she suspected Rafaelo was ranting about. Three volumes. Bound in black leather. Penned in black ink in a stylish sloping hand. A learned man's handwriting. Probably a monk's writing. Possibly Rafaelo's great-great-uncle's handwriting.

She opened her mouth. Phillip lifted his head and caught her eye. She closed her mouth.

Right now those volumes lay in her possession. In her bedside drawer to be precise. Her stomach heaved. Why was Phillip obfuscating? Could it be true? Had Phillip Saxon stolen the works from a young, impressionable woman? Was it possible that Phillip had seduced Maria only for the diaries?

Caitlyn didn't want to think about it. It was too awful. But Phillip's life's passion had been his fascination with creating a fortified wine that would win international awards and respect— it was a vision he'd ignited in Caitlyn when she'd started working at Saxon's Folly as a raw student.

The sound of a snort of disgust roused her from her uneasy reflections.

"If this share that you claim belongs to you is based on the fortune we supposedly make from sherry, then you're sadly misinformed," Heath said. "With the increase in taxes on fortified wines, it's hardly a prize worth pursuing. My father and I have had differences of opinion over his stubborn persistence in continuing down this road before."

The sick feeling in Caitlyn's stomach intensified. Along with guilt. Because she'd shared Phillip's obsessive interest. They'd discussed...dreamed...of buying a tract of land in the Jerez region of Spain, of producing a blend that could be properly labelled and sold as sherry. It would be a winner.

"Or perhaps it's nothing more than an opportunistic get-rich-quick scheme?" Heath's voice was filled with derision.

The Spaniard drew himself up, his gaze turning to black ice. "I don't need a get-rich-quick scheme. I am the Marques de Las Carreras."

Megan gasped. "The Marques de Las Carreras? Then you spoke about *manzanilla* sherry at a show in Paris—"

Rafaelo switched his gaze to the youngest Saxon. "Yes, we met briefly."

"I congratulated you on the silver medals your estate attained for the world-renowned fresh, light *manzanilla* sherry you produce."

Rafaelo nodded. "Unfortunately not quite as magnificent as the Saxon's Folly *fino* product."

Joshua was frowning. "So if it's not a question of money, what do you really want?"

"I want him—" Rafaelo nodded his head toward Phillip without sparing him a glance "—to make good the wrong he did me—and my mother." He slid off the window seat and dusted off his hands. "I want a proportionate share of Saxon's Folly—and, as the eldest son, I would expect an additional portion. And I want Fernando's journals back."

Four

"Have you no pity?" Caitlyn caught up to Rafaelo as he strode out into the blinding sunlight. She shuddered at the memory of the uproar that had erupted after Rafaelo's demand. He'd simply looked down his nose and told the Saxons that his lawyers would be in touch. "The Saxons are grieving."

Rafaelo didn't answer as she bowled along beside him, her long legs easily keeping up with him.

"If it's revenge that you're after, you're making a massive mistake. The biggest loser will be you."

He stopped and swivelled around to face her.

"How can I lose?" Thankfully the black void had gone. The fire was back snapping in his eyes. "And what if I do want revenge? After what that bastard did to my mother, I'm entitled to it."

Caitlyn blinked at the virulence in his tone.

"It's not about whether you're entitled to the satisfaction it brings you, Rafaelo," she said finally. "It's about whether you can let it go."

"I'm not listening to this mumbo jumbo. I will have my revenge. I will get my share in Saxon's Folly—and then I will sell it."

"Sell it?"

"Yes, sell it."

Caitlyn stared at him aghast at the utter finality in his voice. This, then, was what he'd come for. And he'd ruthlessly honed in on the Achilles' heel of the Saxon family. "The Saxons have always kept control of the business. They've fought off attempts by conglomerates to buy them out. You *can't* do this."

He gave her an evil smile. "Just watch me."

His timing was perfect. There had never been a better time to destroy the Saxons. It would take time for the family to regroup after the shock of Roland's death. Time that they didn't have…if Rafaelo made good on his threat.

Couldn't he see what he was doing—what he was destroying? *He couldn't do this.* A sense of calm settled over her. Caitlyn squared her shoulders, her spine stiff and straight and stared him down. "I won't let you do this."

His gaze was implacable, revealing no emotion. "I never expected you to say anything else, *Ms.* Ross. You're on their side."

Rafaelo could see that Caitlyn Ross was fighting not to argue with him. Her shoulders rose and fell under the ridiculous over-sized sports shirt that served only to emphasise her slender femininity. The slim column of her throat framed by the crisp white collar, her wrists so narrow under the banded cuffs.

He watched in silence as she released her breath in a shaky sigh. So she'd seen the wisdom of refraining from arguing—but the effort to remain mute was costing her dearly.

"Nothing to say?" he raised an eyebrow and suppressed a triumphant smile when she gave him a searing look.

"Plenty," she said from between tightly gritted teeth, "but I'm trying not to antagonise you."

Her honesty surprised a shout of laughter from him. "Why hold back? You've been forthright until now. Say what you think."

"But where has it gotten me?" she asked. "All I've done is make everything worse. Because of me Kay's hurting—"

"She would've found out." His mouth slanted. "The appearance of a bastard son is hard to hide."

"Thanks for that." But her expression remained tight.

Rafaelo wanted the sparkle back. "Come, heckle me, tell me what you were going to say."

"You think I'm too outspoken, don't you?"

"It's refreshing." He couldn't tell her that few people—much less women—argued with him these days. That would sound conceited. It was clear she already considered him an arrogant, entitled bastard.

"Tell me what you wanted to say. Would it have antagonised me? Or did you want something from me?" He added the last with a certain degree of wearied resignation.

Most women wanted something from him—marriage, his title, his wealth. A life of indolent luxury as Marquesa de Las Carreras. Even those who gave up on the wedding ring and settled for a skirmish in his bed, expected to be lavishly showered with jewels and clothes and to be royally entertained during their tenure as his mistress.

When had it all grown so tedious?

When had he given up hope of finding a woman who loved him for who he, Rafaelo, was?

"What do I want from you?" Her gaze locked with his, scorching him with the impact. "I want you to reconsider what you intend to do."

"You mean give up the share that's rightfully mine?" he objected, disconcerted by the glow of those peculiarly translucent eyes.

"No, no. I can understand you wanting a share in all this—" she waved a hand to encompass their surroundings "—in the wealth, the family, the land, the beauty that is Saxon's Folly. I don't expect you to forfeit that. And I'm sure you'll be able to work something out with the Saxons. But don't sell it. Stay. Get to know your family—"

"I'm a busy man—I don't have time to take off."

"What's a month? Or even a couple of weeks? You've got years ahead of you." She looked like she was about to stamp her foot. "Darn it, they're your flesh and blood, Rafaelo. Your family. And if you can't do that, can't forget about your thirst for revenge, then go catch that airplane this evening."

Was she daring him? He stared at Caitlyn. No, she couldn't be. She didn't understand who, what, he was. She didn't know about the huge estate, Torres Carreras, he owned in Spain. She didn't know about the power he commanded. She only saw him as a threat to her beloved Saxons. Nothing more.

He'd never met anyone like her.

She didn't seek engagement rings or glittering baubles. She wanted nothing monetary from him. He had a suspicion if he turned and vanished into the ether and never returned she would be relieved.

The realization came as a shock. It had been a very long time since he'd met someone who didn't demand something material from him. All she asked was that he befriend his father—his half siblings—or, if he couldn't do that, she expected him to leave.

What she wanted was selfless—for the Saxons.

But he couldn't oblige. But she needn't know that. Yet. "I'm no longer leaving this evening. I changed my flight booking."

But she wasn't fooled. Rafaelo read the disappointment that clouded her exquisite eyes. She knew that he was staying because he wanted his share of Saxon's Folly with a driving lust. Not because he needed it. But because of what it represented, the chance to set right the wrong that had been done to his mother…to Fernando's memory.

Rafaelo suspected she even understood that he wanted the satisfaction of watching Phillip's face when he broke the news that he'd sold his share to the first bidder. Caitlyn Ross saw what others didn't. She'd known he wanted revenge.

To his astonishment he found himself saying, "If I do as you want, if I extend my stay from a couple of days to a couple of weeks will you have dinner with me?"

A stillness came over her and a frostiness descended around her. "That's not fair!"

"Why not? If I stay, I'll be doing what you want—and I'll be doing something I don't want to do."

Her eyes went from cloudy to utterly opaque, blanking out all emotion. "It's not that I don't want to have dinner with you…. I don't date."

Rafaelo was puzzled by her response. Annoyed, too, his pride affronted. Women didn't turn him down when he invited them out. Usually they leapt all over him. *Yes, Rafaelo. Whatever you want, Rafaelo. Do you want it now or later, Rafaelo?* Instead Caitlyn was edging away. So what in the devil's name was this about?

"Don't date?" He looked her up and down. "But why not? You're an attractive, nubile young woman."

She coloured and looked away, then said softly, "I don't talk about it, either."

Her closed expression warned him to tread carefully. It had to be about her romantic mooning over his dumb-ass half brother. Rafaelo's annoyance grew. "Is it because of what you think you feel for Heath?"

The look she gave him was horrified. "What do you mean?"

Rafaelo waited.

At last she said, "It has nothing to do with Heath." She gave a broken little laugh. "How can it? Your brother doesn't even know I exist."

"Half brother," he corrected. "He's a fool. And so are you for pining over one man. *Madre de Dios*—" he raked a hand through his hair "—how long has this been going on?"

She spread her hands helplessly. "It's complicated. You don't—can't ever—understand."

"So I'm a simpleton?"

"No…no. Please, I'm not insulting your intelligence. It's my fault."

Mouth twisting with wry humour, he murmured, "Ah, this is one of those circumstances where a modern woman would say, 'It's not you, it's me,' hmm?" The consternation in her eyes made him regret the impulse to tease her. Almost. He made one of the lightning-fast decisions that he was famed for. "I'll stay. Two weeks. I'll extend my booking in town."

"No!" At his look of surprise she tempered her tone. "You can't possibly stay in a hotel. There are three guest cottages on the estate. I'm sure you can stay in one of them."

"All right."

Her face lit up, as if he'd promised her Christmas.

Rafaelo gazed into her pale eyes. They should have been cold and wintry. They ought to have frozen out this *loco* attraction. Instead they sparkled like clear, pure crystal, radiating enthusiasm and pleasure, drawing him deeper under her spell.

With a struggle he found his voice. "Don't read too much into all this."

"I understand," she said at last. "You're still going to sell your share in Saxon's Folly."

"And don't think you'll change my mind," he growled.

Several days later Caitlyn let out a tired sigh. The path that led over the gentle hill from the winery to the stables, where she lived in a loft apartment, seemed longer and bumpier than usual. Her hot, tired feet dragged.

In the distance the golden glow of the late-afternoon sunlight cast a creamy glaze over the whitewashed stables. To the left, a ray of sun glinted off the chrome trim of Joshua Saxon's Range Rover, where he inspected the vines. At the end of the block a copse of native trees marked the start of rolling grass meadows dotted with horses, some grazing, others slumbering, heads low, tails whisking to keep the flies at bay.

It had been hellish in the winery. Surrounded by oak casks, Caitlyn had spent the day racking wine, transferring it from one cask to another to remove the lees. She'd worked quickly to lessen the exposure to air. Her back ached and her feet were hot and sore in the scuffed sneakers. She longed for the sharp needles of a cool, refreshing shower…followed by a good book and her own company for a while.

Except today was Thursday. Family night. The night the Saxons all made a point of having dinner together—and included regulars as part of the extended family. Caitlyn was one of those regulars. Even Amy, Roland's grief-stricken fiancée, would be there. Since Kay had reluctantly agreed that Rafaelo could stay in one of the vineyard cottages, it was possible Rafaelo would have received an invitation to dinner, too.

If the Spaniard was there, the Saxons would need all the support they could muster, she couldn't abandon them. Caitlyn glanced down, caught sight of her jeans and wrinkled her nose. Kicking a stone out of her path, she decided that solitude and the best seller she was reading would have to wait. But a shower was a necessity—along with a clean change of jeans—before she'd be respectable enough to grace anyone's dinner table.

The sound of whistling gave her pause. Her head came up. She searched and located Rafaelo lounging on a tussock just inside a paddock near the stable block, his back propped up against the fence post, his harsh profile softened by lips pursed to whistle. Caitlyn couldn't help noticing that his overlong hair gleamed blue-black like Tui feathers in the sun. She slowed, her heartbeat accelerating with the discomforting awareness that the sight of Rafaelo brought.

She looked away.

Lady Killer was standing a distance away, ears flickering back and forth, the muscles in his haunches bunched and his tail tucked between his legs, every line of his body screaming his protest at the human invading his space.

"Come, sit." Voice low, Rafaelo patted the mound of grass beside him.

Her pulse went wild. She could no longer pretend she hadn't spotted him and sneak past. "I thought you were sleeping."

He cracked one eye open. "That's what I wanted the stallion to think."

"He hates people, that horse." Caitlyn drew nearer and folded her arms across the top railing of the fence, propping her chin on her forearm. At the sound of her voice, the stallion's ears flattened against his skull.

Rafaelo continued to whistle, a slow mesmerizing sound. Lady Killer stood, stiff-legged, not grazing, his tension showing his fury and his resentment.

Eyes half-closed, the Spaniard murmured, "Sit down. You're threatening him by standing there."

"Me? Threatening *him?*" Caitlyn gave a snort of disbelieving laughter and glanced nervously to the patch of grass Rafaelo was patting.

Taking in Rafaelo's long, relaxed body reclining on the invitingly green grass, his lazy gaze focused on the horse, she decided that the man was no threat to her. Bent double, she stepped through between the railings and lowered her tired, aching body beside Rafaelo.

He didn't react. A fantail twittered and fluttered crazily in a nearby bush. Gradually the tension leached from Caitlyn's muscles. It was heaven to rest back on her elbows and inhale the fresh scent of crushed grass.

Rafaelo didn't even open his eyes to spare her a glance. Caitlyn snatched up the opportunity to examine him. The hawkish profile, the sensually pursed lips, the olive skin stretched tight across his cheekbones, the small jagged scar beneath his mouth. He was too male to ever be called beautiful.

Then it came to her. The perfect word to describe him.

Macho.

"He's not as tough as he'd have everyone believe." At his words, she turned her attention back to the horse.

"Ha! Don't believe that. There's a reason he's called Lady Killer—and it's not because of his flirty ways with the mares," she muttered darkly.

"He's not a killer. He's an Andalusian," Rafaelo continued. "In my country we value such horses. We care for them and train them. We do not leave them to become wild and wary like this stallion."

"He hasn't been abandoned," she protested. "Roland bought him about four months before his death. He had plans to turn him into a dressage horse. But the horse is difficult. And with all the work at the winery, Roland didn't have enough time to put into him. Then he died."

"Someone needs to take the horse in hand."

"No one has the time."

"Or the interest." Rafaelo's voice was flat. "I have two weeks. I will speak to my father. Someone needs to give that animal time."

Caitlyn glanced at him in shock. He was no longer pretending to sleep; all his attention was fixed on the stallion. Caitlyn had been furious with him for pursuing his plan for revenge, to wrest a piece of Saxon's Folly away from the Saxons. But perhaps it had cooled his anger. It was certainly the first time she'd heard him refer to Phillip as "my father." She suspected Phillip would be relieved to have Rafaelo's time occupied, preventing him from skulking around the winery, poking around the fortified wines that they produced. But contrarily she said, "It will be a waste of time. No one can catch that horse, he leads them a fine dance. Jim simply opens his door in the morning and shoos him into the paddock, leaving him a hay net for the day. In the evening, we open his stable door and he comes in for his evening meal."

The eyes that connected with hers were frighteningly direct. "Who is Jim?"

"One of the cellar hands. He helps Megan feed the horses and muck out the stalls in the morning. Although some students from the local polytechnic who do their practical coursework here also help. And so do I when Megan's overseas at a wine show."

"You can ride?"

"Yep, I usually exercise Breeze when Megan's away." She pointed to a pretty chestnut mare in the next field. Under his intent gaze the tingling returned, and she moved restlessly. "What can you do with the stallion in two weeks?"

He shrugged. "Teach him to trust me."

"No chance. That horse doesn't trust anyone."

"He already knows I won't hurt him."

"Hurt him?" She gave a disbelieving laugh. "If anyone is going to do hurting, it's that mad creature."

"He's not mad, he's scared."

She stared at him. "Scared? How do you work that out?"

He didn't turn his head. His profile was harsh and jagged against the verdant grass and the foliage of the surrounding trees. "The first time I raised my arm, he squealed and kicked and tried to bite me. Now, when I raise it, he flinches and puts his ears flat. Someone has hit this horse around the head." There was cold fury in Rafaelo's voice.

"It wasn't any of the Saxons." Caitlyn sprang to their defence. "He was already difficult when Roland bought him."

"Stop worrying. I don't suspect your precious Saxons. But it angers me that a good animal has been ruined by someone's uncontrollable anger."

Caitlyn fell silent. She perused him, a new respect filling her. His strength and power was clearly visible in his long, whipcord body and inflexible will, yet he was gentle, too. She didn't want to examine why that moved her so profoundly.

"Does anyone groom the stallion?" he asked.

Caitlyn focused on the horse with relief. "Not since he trapped Jim between those powerful hindquarters and the wall and aimed a vicious kick at his head. Jim was lucky to clamber up the wall out of the way."

Rafaelo fell silent.

The fantail was still twittering and over near the stables Caitlyn saw that a pair of swallows had appeared in the evening sky—the first she'd seen this season.

Rafaelo spoke suddenly, "I'll make you a deal. Dinner in town says that within a week I'll have that horse caught, groomed and eating out my hand."

"Loser pays?" Caitlyn started to laugh. There was no chance that Rafaelo was even going to get near the horse. "You better bring your wallet."

"I don't intend to lose." He threw her a narrow-eyed look that stirred the flutter of butterflies in her stomach and caused her laughter to die. Then he smiled, a wide white grin that sparkled with victory, causing adrenaline to jolt through her.

"I'll do that," he said softly, "we've got a date."

Too late she saw the trap. Caitlyn stared at him. Win or lose, she was committed to an evening out with him.

Great going for a woman who didn't date.

Five

An hour later, scrubbed and clean, Caitlyn pushed back the heavy drapes and stepped through the French doors into the formal salon of the Saxon homestead. She stopped at the sight of Phillip and Rafaelo eyeing each other across the wide expanse of a magnificent Persian rug like a pair of wary wolves.

Both men turned to her, relief in two sets of dark eyes. The tension eased a little when Caitlyn started prattling about Lady Killer. A first. Normally the mere mention of the stallion's name was enough to cause dissent, but for once Phillip appeared to welcome the topic and soon the men were debating whether the stallion could be turned into a dressage horse.

Caitlyn fell silent, watching Rafaelo warily. She hadn't forgotten how easily he had lulled her into a sense of false security earlier. Her wariness increased when she caught Rafaelo's hooded eyes scanning the room as he examined the paintings, the furniture, the jewelled hues of the acres of Persian carpet underfoot that contrasted with the polished kauri floorboards.

Was he calculating the value of what his share in the immense historic Victorian homestead might be worth?

"Just be careful," Phillip was saying, "that bloody horse caused an accident last month. Alyssa was badly hurt."

"Do I hear my name?" Alyssa picked that moment to enter the salon, Joshua at her side. Sleek and sophisticated, she was wearing a burnt amber dress that suited her dramatic beauty and dark red hair.

By comparison Caitlyn felt underdressed in denims faded almost to white and not even her newest sneakers and the black tank top she wore eased the sensation. Then she shrugged the discomfort away. Joshua was wearing jeans, too. There was no expectation to dress for dinner at Saxon's Folly. There never had been. The Saxons might be wealthy, but they weren't pretentious.

"We're talking about your fall," Caitlyn said, remembering that awful moment when Alyssa had lain on the cobbles in the stable yard, so still and so pale, Joshua kneeling beside her, his eyes wide with panic.

For one horrible moment Caitlyn had thought Alyssa was dead—and so had a devastated Joshua. The memory still made Caitlyn's skin crawl.

"My hand hardly hurts anymore." Alyssa held up her hand, showing off a narrow bandage. "The physiotherapist says I'm well on the mend, I just need to keep doing my exercises."

"I should've shot that stallion." Joshua put an arm around Alyssa and pulled her close.

"It wasn't his fault," Alyssa protested, huddled against his chest.

"Alyssa was riding the stallion?" Rafaelo looked surprised.

"No, no," said Caitlyn. "She was riding Breeze. Two kids were lurking behind the trees in the paddock. Lady Killer—"

"I do not like that name," Rafaelo interjected. "It makes the horse sound like a murderer."

"He damn nearly killed Alyssa."

"Nonsense, Josh, I'm fine," said Alyssa.

Joshua brushed his cheek against Alyssa's hair, his expression bemused. Alyssa smiled up at him, love in her eyes, the rest of the company forgotten. Caitlyn couldn't stop the melting sensation that filled her at the sight of them together. This was the kind of love that she'd once dreamed of finding...one day.

Little chance of that now...

Finally, Joshua said, "He's a Devil Horse."

"Then call him Diablo, it's better than Lady Killer," Rafaelo suggested. He inclined his head to Alyssa. "I apologise for interrupting your account."

Caitlyn took over the story as Joshua placed a kiss on Alyssa's temple. "When Joshua and Alyssa arrived back from their ride, Lady Killer...Diablo," she amended at Rafaelo's hard stare, "was in a right royal lather with those hoodlums in his paddock. They made a dash for it. At the roar of the motorbike, Breeze bolted."

"Alyssa fell badly and needed treatment for her hand," Phillip added. "I'll accept that particular incident might not have been the stallion's fault, but what he did to Jim—trapping him in the corner of the stable—was downright mean. If anything like that happens again, I'm going to have him destroyed."

"Let me see what I can do with the horse first," Rafaelo cut in.

"Take care." Phillip appraised Rafaelo's height, his broad shoulders. "If you can master him, as far as I'm concerned you can have him."

Rafaelo looked startled. Then his features hardened into a determined mask. He started to say something, but paused as Kay entered the salon, Megan close behind her. With a frown Caitlyn noticed that Kay was wearing a dressy skirt. When had the dress code for these Thursday-night family dinners changed? The crease between her brows smoothed when she saw that Megan still wore work clothes.

"Dinner will be another fifteen minutes," Kay announced.

"Looks like we're all here." Kay scanned the gathering. She barely glanced at Phillip and her expression clouded over as her gaze rested briefly on Rafaelo. Caitlyn sensed the older woman's pain at being faced with such incontrovertible evidence of her husband's infidelity. The lines around the older woman's eyes had deepened since Rafaelo's arrival—and the revelation of Phillip's betrayal.

"Amy's not here," said Caitlyn, more to distract Kay's attention from Rafaelo than for any other reason.

"No, she didn't feel up to it." Shadows shifted in Kay's eyes. "It's been quite a week."

That was an understatement. Kay must be thinking of Roland's memorial service…of her dead son.

"Heath hasn't arrived yet. He's late. Again." Phillip's tone was riddled with censure.

Kay looked even more upset.

In an effort to head off an argument between Phillip and Kay, Caitlyn said, "If his day was as crazy as mine, he probably finished work not long ago." Her swift defence of Heath earned her a narrow-eyed stare from Rafaelo that caused her stomach to dip and roll.

"He's late. Stop making excuses for him, Caitlyn." Phillip's bushy eyebrows lowered. "Now, why don't we sit down in comfort while we wait for my tardy son to arrive." He gestured to the pair of sofas that faced each other. "Can I get anyone a predinner drink?"

Joshua collapsed into an armchair and Alyssa perched on the arm, while Megan settled herself in a navy brocade armchair that had always been Roland's spot. A pang of sadness shook Caitlyn. Roland was sorely missed. Joshua must've had the same thought because his hand slid over Alyssa's in a way that could only be described as comforting.

Caitlyn made for one of the sofas.

"Would you like a glass of sauvignon blanc or sherry?" Phillip asked Caitlyn.

"Sherry, please."

Rafaelo sank down beside her on the sofa. Caitlyn stilled, instantly aware of his overwhelming, breathtaking masculinity. Then she turned to him and said in a cheerfully polite voice, "You must taste *Flores Fino*. It's a Saxon's Folly favourite."

"I'll try the white wine." Rafaelo's lips were tight. "So, you call it sherry here, do you?"

Uh-oh. Detecting tension, she picked her words carefully. "Habit. The label doesn't refer to sherry—it describes it only as *Flores Fino*. But in the style what we produce is Spanish *fino*, based on—"

"Based on?"

Based on his great-uncle's process.

She shook her head and took a quick sip from the glass that Phillip handed her. Despite the sweetness of the amber liquid, her mouth tasted bitter. Rafaelo had come not only to seek vengeance on his mother's behalf but also because he believed that Phillip had stolen his great-great-uncle Fernando's journals. Yet after that dreadful confrontation in Phillip's office, Phillip had pulled her aside to explain that he'd bought the journals from Maria before swearing Caitlyn to silence. He didn't want Rafaelo getting his hands on the journals—or the magic methods they recorded.

To her relief Rafaelo didn't demand an answer. Instead he asked, "That is *Flores Fino*, yes?"

Her heart thudding with anxiety, she ran her tongue over dry lips, her mind blank. Finally she nodded.

"The first time I tasted *Flores Fino*—" Rafaelo nodded toward her glass "—I was, how do you say, blown away? It was what I had been trying to achieve for years. As a child my mother told me tales of the sherry my great-great-uncle had made. She tried to remember what she'd read in the journals." He gave Phillip a dark look. "She'd jotted down some short notes in her diary, the notes of a history student, not a winemaker. But, helped by my fa—by the Marques—they gave me a start."

Caitlyn swallowed, distressed by the longing in his eyes.

"I wanted to produce a *fino* sherry like that. A sherry that would've made my great-great-uncle proud." An air of poignant longing clung to him. Then he shook himself and it vanished. "Instead I tasted that in France. Everyone was excited by the out-standing quality. It was like tasting the nectar of the gods. Per-fection." Rafaelo gave her a sidelong glance that made her heart sink still farther. "I noted the makers. Ross and Saxon. And admired—yearned for—their talent."

Caitlyn suspected she knew where this would end. "Rafaelo—"

"But it wasn't God-given talent, was it?" There was a rawness to his harsh tone. "I cannot tell you what I felt when my father—the Marques—revealed that my real father was Phillip Saxon." His eyes were flat and empty, all the energy and spark gone. "It was as if the missing piece to the puzzle had been dropped into my lap. I hardly needed to hear the story that my mother wished to tell. Because I knew."

Caitlyn waited, dry-mouthed.

"I knew instantly that the nectar I had tasted was too similar to the notes my mother had given me. I knew…" His voice trailed away as Phillip came closer. Looking from Caitlyn to Phillip, he asked with a hard edge, "So who is the expert then?"

In the manner of a true academic Caitlyn had been fascinated by the leather-bound volumes. She'd fished the dusty journals off the bookshelves and had read them, cover to cover. It had fired her up. She had seen the possibilities.

"I've always made sherry," Phillip said, trying to look modest, and Caitlyn's shoulders sagged. "Caitlyn worked with me when she first came, but once Heath left she had so much else to do."

For a moment annoyance at the dismissal of her role in establishing Saxon's Folly as a top producer of fortified wines overcame her relief. Then she caught sight of the fury in Rafaelo's face and she wanted to cry. Rafaelo believed Phillip's skill came from Fernando's journals—the very journals he believed Phillip had stolen from his mother. Phillip's attitude would do nothing to dampen Rafaelo's desire for revenge. Did Phillip not realise that far from establishing himself as a figure of admiration in Rafaelo's eyes, he was simply alienating, enraging, his firstborn son more?

Finally she compromised. Let Phillip have his pride, but she had to take responsibility, too. "Phillip has always been my mentor—it was something we were both fascinated by. But it's true that since Heath bought Amy's father's estate on the other side of The Divide and ceased to be Saxon's Folly's winemaker, I've had less time for sherry."

"Heath should never have left," Phillip muttered.

Across from them, Joshua started to frown.

"Too many things we couldn't agree on, Dad," Heath said quietly from the doorway. "And I will have sherry, thanks."

"You're late," Phillip said gruffly.

"Mother told me that Amy wasn't coming this evening. I stopped in on my way here to see if she was okay."

"It would've done her good to get out for the evening." Kay shook her head sadly. "She hasn't been at work the whole week."

"She looked so pale and unhappy the last three weeks, I think it's better that she's taken some time off." Megan looked troubled. "I don't think she ever grieved properly after Roland's death. She was so busy trying to cheer us up…and pick up the slack at the winery."

Heath came closer. "I tried to talk her into coming tonight— she didn't want to. Hell, I can't even get through to her right now." Frustration simmered in Heath's eyes. "Everything I suggest, she resists."

"Should I talk to her?" Joshua looked around at the others, his gaze alighting longest on Alyssa. "Will that help?"

Heath hesitated. "Maybe."

"Both of you need to back off and give her time. She's lost the man she loves." Alyssa turned her hand and threaded her fingers through Joshua's and squeezed. "In her shoes I'd be heartbroken."

"That she is." Heath collapsed on the sofa facing them, and Caitlyn decided that he looked even more weary than she felt. It was a terrible time for Heath, Megan and Joshua. Their brother's death, the shocking discovery of Rafaelo's existence and learning of their father's betrayal of their mother all meant that everyone's nerves were stretched to the breaking point.

Caitlyn wished that the clock could be turned back and everything made right.

Ivy arrived bearing a tray and offered around dainty glasses filled with amber-coloured sherry and glasses of pale gold sauvignon blanc.

Rafaelo bent forward to set down his glass of wine as Ivy departed.

"Wait." Caitlyn touched his arm. "Don't put it there."

He stared down at her hand on his arm, then lifted his gaze to meet hers. The impact was like a burst of static. From his raised eyebrow, Caitlyn knew he'd felt it, too.

His skin felt hot under her touch. Caitlyn started to snatch her hand away. Then stopped. No, darn it. She was a respected award-winning winemaker. What was she doing jumping away from a man's bare skin like some terrified little virgin?

So she left her hand on his arm and returned his stare. The contact was electrifying. Under her fingertips she felt the muscles contract. His eyes grew blacker than midnight.

All of the sudden Caitlyn had a sense of getting in deeper than she'd ever been before. For a cowardly moment she half wished she had withdrawn her hand, when she'd had the chance, but now that moment had passed.

Irrevocably.

He smiled, and said so softly that only she could hear, "I'm getting used to your telling me what to do."

She blushed. "Sorry, I didn't mean to. That table has been in Kay's family for centuries. I wanted to set down a coaster—" Caitlyn reached for a hand-painted box and extracted a pile of glass coasters, setting them out on the low table that separated the two long sofas. "I don't want it to be marked from the glasses."

"I'm surprised Kay places the table where it could risk getting damaged."

"She likes to surround herself with possessions with meaning. I don't think she'd mind it being marked—she'd see that as part of the beauty."

"But you're protecting her from heartache?"

"Yes. The Saxon family has been very good to me. It's my turn to protect them. Wouldn't you—if you were in the same position?"

Their eyes held for a long moment and a beat of perfect understanding arched between them.

Phillip's voice broke in, "What do you think of the sherry, Heath?"

Heath lifted the sherry glass and sipped. "Very good."

"It's more than good. It's a winner," said Phillip argumentatively. But Heath didn't respond. "Sure you don't want a taste, Rafaelo?"

"Quite sure." Rafaelo's tone was measured and frighteningly formal, his curved lips compressed into that hard line that caused Caitlyn to shiver.

She gave Phillip a quick look. He was so caught up in his battle with Heath that he didn't seem to sense that he was antagonizing Rafaelo. Couldn't he fathom that the sherry was a volatile topic tied up with Rafaelo's complicated relationship with his family? The mother, her great-uncle and the father to whom Rafaelo believed he owed his loyalty. She wished Phillip would shut up.

Heath stretched out his legs—jean-clad Caitlyn noticed with relief—and addressed Rafaelo, "That's where my path diverges from my father's. I'm not a trophy hunter, I simply make solid no-fuss wines to drink with meals."

"Don't pay attention to him." Joshua tipped his head sideways against the back of the armchair. "The wines he produces are superb—far from no-fuss."

"You should taste them, Rafaelo, they're fabulous." Caitlyn ran interference again, watching the byplay between the Saxon males and trying to fathom the underlying currents.

"Thank you for that endorsement, kitten," Heath said.

"Kitten?" Rafaelo's lip curled in disgust. *"Kitten?"*

"My nickname," said Caitlyn, very quickly. She flashed Heath a half smile, wishing that the undercurrents would evaporate.

Even Joshua's eyes narrowed, revealing his awareness of the rising tension in the room despite his outwardly relaxed appearance. On the other side of the room, Kay was chewing her lip, her eyes flitting from her husband to the Spanish interloper to her younger son—clearly Kay was worried, too.

And beside her Rafaelo felt like a powder keg about to explode.

In the golden glow of the tall candles, Rafaelo studied the straw-coloured wine in the Baccarat glass, then he glanced over the top to where Caitlyn sat beside him, her meal finished, too.

Kitten!

Rafaelo suppressed a snort. Heath had it wrong. This woman was no kitten. His half brother didn't know her. He drew comfort from that thought. She turned her head. Her eyes, the colour of pale, unearthly crystal, so clear, so pure, connected with his. Desire jolted through him.

She reminded him of a wolf. Fiercely protective. Her eyes glowing, all-seeing, uncanny in the candlelight.

"What do you think?"

He stared at her. What did he think? *Madre de Dios,* he couldn't think. Not while her eyes transfixed him, entrapped him in their clear depths.

"Would you prefer red?"

She was talking about the wine, he realised belatedly, jerking himself back to reality, to the glass in front of him, to the dining room in the Saxon homestead, and to the conversation dominated by weather and Brix.

A conversation that he would normally command. But not tonight. Tonight turbulence raged within him. He sensed resentment from his half siblings. Not that he blamed them. Anger lingered against Phillip—his dishonourable father—who blatantly offered around sherry, boasted about the awards he'd garnered, from a process he had stolen from a vulnerable, loving woman. Some of his dark emotion spilled onto Caitlyn; her name had been listed alongside Phillip Saxon's as winemaker.

He pushed himself to his feet. "Excuse me, please." Rafaelo stalked to the tall doors that led outside. For the first time in years he craved a cigarette. But he'd given them up a decade ago. He felt her presence before she stepped outside.

"I needed a breath of fresh air," he felt compelled to explain.

Then Caitlyn smiled and the blackness eased inside him. Rafaelo told himself that he was being too harsh. She'd been an employee, acting under instructions… Phillip Saxon's instructions. And the desire for her that had been tamped down ignited again.

"So how did you come to work for Saxon's Folly?" he asked Caitlyn to get his head out of that dark black pit it was stuck in.

"Heath tutored me during my first year at university—we became friends. He organised a vacation job for me at Saxon's

Folly. After I finished studying, the family offered me a full-time position as a cellar hand." And she'd always wondered what had motivated that offer.

Rafaelo tilted his head sideways studying her. "What made Heath single you out?"

"He's a kind man. I think he felt sorry for me." Caitlyn laughed without humour.

Sorry for her? What was wrong with the man? Rafaelo wondered. "But why?"

She hesitated. "I was a swot."

"A swot?" Rafaelo asked, puzzled by the word.

"I studied too much. I came out of university with a first class honours degree, a willingness to learn and not much else. I always had my nose in a book."

"Ah." Had she seized the opportunity to work at Saxon's Folly because of Heath Saxon? Such a smart woman, so besotted over such a dumb ass.

Through the glass doors, Rafaelo cast his clueless half brother a damning look. Didn't he see under the worn jeans and sneakers to the woman she was?

"Heath was already winemaker here," Caitlyn was saying. "He'd taken over from Phillip, who had worked at a killing pace for the past ten years and wanted to start slowing down. Joshua studied locally and ran the vineyards, while Roland looked after the marketing side."

"That was around the time he—" Rafaelo couldn't bring himself to use Saxon's name "—decided to give his sons shares equal to those that his wife held in Saxon's Folly, while retaining the largest share himself." Only to the legitimate sons, of course.

Caitlyn's eyes widened in surprise.

"I made it my business to find out such things," he said in reply to her unanswered question.

"He gave Megan a share equal to her brothers'."

"Only later, once she'd finished her studies."

"She was younger." Caitlyn came instantly to Phillip Saxon's defence.

"So why did Heath leave Saxon's Folly?" That was one question Rafaelo wanted answered.

Caitlyn lifted her shoulders in a small movement and let them drop. "Heath and Phillip had had a bitter fallout. I was assistant winemaker by that time. Heath suggested that Phillip and Kay offer me the top job, winemaker at Saxon's Folly."

He read the pride in her eyes, the disbelief that still lingered. "Didn't you think you could do it?"

"It had been my secret dream, so deeply buried that I never saw any chance of it coming true."

"Especially not with a Saxon already in the winemaker role," he said drily. "You needed Heath to move on."

"I never wanted that!" Her eyes sparked with anger. "That's a horrid thing to imply. Heath's always been fantastic to me. Supportive, encouraging. I…" Her voice trailed away.

Rafaelo didn't need her help to join the dots.

Caitlyn shook her head. "Oh, what's the use of trying to explain? You'll never understand."

He understood. More than she thought. She fancied herself in love with Heath Saxon.

Caitlyn saw his mouth tighten. She wished he could get over this stupid antagonism that he and Heath shared.

How could she explain what it had meant to her to be promoted to chief winemaker? That had been Mount Olympus back then. Attaining such lofty heights had seemed more far-fetched than the hope of catching Heath's attention—a dream which she was starting to realise had been nothing more than the crush of a bookish late developer. She turned away from Rafaelo, unwilling to think about what had prompted such a ground-shifting revelation, and made for the tall glass doors.

"I'm going back inside." After a long moment, she heard him follow and tried to tell herself that she didn't care what he did— as long as he didn't harm the Saxons.

Later, after murmuring farewells to Phillip and Kay, Caitlyn glanced to where Rafaelo stood listening to Alyssa and Joshua argue about whether Saxon's Folly should be sponsoring a newly created food and wine TV show. Since their conversation, Rafaelo hadn't said much. Hell, he'd even declined dessert—no one ever refused a helping of Ivy's pavlova.

But then she'd been silent, too, caught up in the discovery that she wasn't in love with Heath Saxon—that it had been nothing more than a very convenient crush that had prevented the need for a boyfriend when she hadn't wanted one. And later…

Well, later it had meant there'd been no pressure on her to come to terms with what had happened.

Her breath hissed out. A whole new world opened ahead of her. One filled with men and passion and all the things she'd spent five years avoiding. She glanced toward Rafaelo.

In one of those freakish tricks of timing, Alyssa and Joshua stopped arguing and looked toward the French doors. Rafaelo's gaze followed. Caitlyn was caught staring. She gave them a little wave and mouthed, "Good night."

Rafaelo came toward her. "I'll walk you home."

"That's not necessary." Caitlyn gave a breathy little laugh. "Goodness, I've walked home often enough. This isn't the city. This is Saxon's Folly, I'm hardly in any danger of getting mugged. If I'd thought that, I'd have called Pita, the guard, to walk me home."

"I thought you might like the company," Rafaelo murmured. "I'm on foot, too. The stables are on my way home."

Coming up behind him, Alyssa said, "Caitlyn's right. Saxon's Folly is as far removed from the city as you can get—ask me, I'm the original fast-lane gal, aren't I?" And she gave Joshua a loving smile that had him hurrying to her side, his dark eyes melting.

For a raw instant Caitlyn felt a tearing of envy. *She* wanted to be loved like that. For a fraction of time she let her gaze rest on Heath, then she swung her attention back to Rafaelo.

His eyes were piercing. Caitlyn felt as if he could see all the way to her soul, to the need that lay there, beneath the frozen wastes.

"Thank you." Her voice sounded strangled. "I'd like you to walk me home."

Rafaelo glanced at Heath and back to her. "Would you?"

Six

Patches of moonlight danced on the pathway as they walked into the copse of tall, whispering trees. The bright light from the homestead receded behind them.

"What did you mean by that crack?"

Caitlyn sounded mad. Rafaelo glanced sideways. Her stride was long, her shoulders thrown back in challenge. No hint of Heath's kitten remained.

Rafaelo didn't pretend to misunderstand. "Heath has been your tutor, your friend, he arranged a job for you. You're in lo—"

She covered her ears with her hands. "Don't say it, please."

He shot her a frustrated glare. "*¡Vale!* I won't. But don't lie to yourself. Instead ask yourself why you're wasting your life? You're young, smart, beautiful. Why long for Heath Saxon? He calls you *kitten,* for heaven's sake." Rafaelo snorted in disgust. "The man doesn't even know your true nature. Find yourself someone else, someone who appreciates you for the woman you are."

Her hands dropped away from her ears back to her side. She didn't want to hear what he'd had to say. The silence told him how much she resented his interference.

No matter. He didn't need to say more. It might be harsh, but it was true.

They walked around a bend, and the trees thinned. Ahead the well-lit stables came into view.

At last Caitlyn spoke. "Is this some sort of crafty attempt to persuade me to desert the Saxons? Some divide-and-rule to get the revenge you crave?"

"Caitlyn—"

"It won't work. Heath has been a good friend. I'll always be grateful to him—he's done so much for me, he even gave me my dream job."

"So in exchange you presented him your heart." Jealousy uncurled within Rafaelo. "What else did you give him? You were young, impressionable, he was older, more experienced… did you feel obliged to give him your virginity in exchange for his tutoring?"

She stopped in her tracks.

"Rafaelo!"

The scandalised shock in her voice was too real to be feigned. A silver moonbeam slanted across her face as she looked up at him. "You make it sound so commercial…like a cold, bloodless transaction. It wasn't like that!"

"So he *did* take your virginity."

She gave a sharp sigh of frustration. "He was my tutor—not my boyfriend. And why suspect Heath? There were a gazillion other guys who were only too keen to initiate first-year students to the joys of sex."

"That's all?" Relief swelled through Rafaelo like a tidal wave, he ignored the fact that Caitlyn had found some other student to love. All that concerned him was Heath Saxon, the man who was in his face every way he turned, the man who was his half brother. "You never slept with him?"

"We became friends. That's all! Heath's never known how I feel about him, so I'd appreciate it if you keep it to yourself."

"You've never touched him like you touched my arm earlier?"

"No!"

"Never felt that bolt of awareness surge between you?"

"Never." Despite the cover of darkness, she averted her face. "You shouldn't be asking me these questions—my love life has got nothing to do with you."

He stopped dead. Grasping her chin, he demanded, "Look at me."

To his immense frustration the dappled moonlight was too dim to reveal her thoughts.

"How can you say it's none of my business? Didn't you feel the charge between us when you touched me earlier? Can't you feel this...*thing* between us?"

"No." She shook her head in fierce denial and her fine silky hair whipped against his arm. "There's nothing between us."

"Don't lie," he said quietly, furious that she could deny this...this...force that seared him.

"Let me go."

Silence.

"Please..." Caitlyn shut her eyes. It was hopeless. Rafaelo wouldn't listen. Her only hope lay in the fact that someone might hear her scream. It was late...dark...the Saxons were all up at the homestead.

"Caitlyn?"

She opened her mouth but couldn't utter a word.

"Caitlyn, look at me, *querida*."

Her eyes snapped open. Rafaelo stood in front of her, still big, still strong. He'd stepped away. He'd released her chin. Now he was frowning down at her. And he didn't look pleased.

"Caitlyn?"

He sounded worried.

"Are you okay?" He didn't take his eyes off her. "Do you want me to call someone? Megan? Or Kay?"

He wanted to call someone? Why?

"Come, let me take you home, you look like you're about to pass out."

She didn't move.

"I'll call the homestead—get Kay or Megan to help you." There was a note of sharp concern in his voice. He already had his cell phone in his hand, the other hand cupped her elbow. No fear flared. She felt only numbness.

She let him lead her to the foot of the black wrought-iron stairwell that led up against the exterior wall to her loft apartment. Heard him hit the buttons on his phone.

"I'm okay," she said. He wasn't going to hurt her.

He glanced at her and stuck the phone in his shirt pocket and hastily pressed her shoulders down, until she sank on the stairs. "You're as white as a ghost. Put your head between your knees."

She obeyed, heard him settle beside her. The panic had begun to recede.

"Do you need something?"

"No, I'll be fine."

His gaze was searching. "Has this happened before?"

Oh, yes. But she had no intention of talking about it.

She rose unsteadily to her feet. "I'd better go upstairs and make myself something to drink. Warm milk will help."

He didn't look convinced. "Can I take you to the doctor?"

"I don't need a doctor." She simply needed to be alone. To have a warm bath and get into bed. Then she'd sleep. She turned away and started to climb the stairs.

"I'll see you in."

Instantly the tension was back. "No… I'll be fine. Really." She drew a deep breath when he started to argue and hurriedly inserted the key in the door.

A last backward glance showed her that the black eyes were sombre as he stood tall and proud and allowed her to close the door in his face.

"So what do you want me to do?"

Caitlyn's impatient retort to Jim made her realise that she was being unreasonable. She took a deep breath, thought about the problem that Jim had come to her with and suggested a solution. Then she went and made herself a cup of tea and took it out into the courtyard to the south of the winery.

The morning had passed in a rush. For once the winery wasn't holding its usual fascination, the blend of art and science not captivating her as it normally did.

It was all Rafaelo's fault.

Embarrassment rolling like nausea in her stomach had woken her several times during the night. She took a sip of tea. He must think she was a nut. No, he thought she suffered from some medical incapacity.

Most likely insanity.

Setting down the mug on the bench beside her, she groaned in humiliation and buried her head in her hands. How was she ever going to face him again?

He'd wanted to kiss her last night.

But he hadn't. Because fear had closed in on her, taking over her, until she'd run to her sanctuary, victim to the terror that crawled through her. Silly, scared little kitten.

Kitten. The joking, childish nickname was suddenly a symptom of all that was wrong.

Was it any wonder that Heath had never viewed her as a woman? Rafaelo had been brutally honest last night, telling her that she was wasting her time on Heath.

Deep down she knew he was right. She needed a life. Yes, she needed a wake-up call. Not because she was sleeping—but because she was frozen. A solid block of ice that only looked like a woman. If she hadn't felt a tinge of bitterness at the waste, she might have found it funny.

But did that mean letting Rafaelo kiss her would be right? He was the cause of this restlessness, the dissatisfaction, the strange discomfort that lay in the base of her stomach, warming her, making her itch. And nothing about that was remotely humorous.

Rafaelo wouldn't hurt her…

Then caution kicked in. How could she know that? She barely knew the man. All she'd seen was the macho exterior, the snapping eyes that hinted at passion and dark depths of emotion beneath the handsome veneer. How could she be sure that he was safe?

Better to keep her distance.

He'd be leaving soon. She only had to keep a lid on her suddenly awakening libido for a week and a half, then he'd be gone. She could do that. But in the meantime he'd be spending all his time messing with a dangerous stallion. The horse had already proved he hated humans. What if Rafaelo got hurt?

It didn't bear thinking about.

The hour before lunchtime crawled. Despite resolving to keep far away from Rafaelo an unexpected worry for the damn man ate at her.

Finally at her lunch break Caitlyn couldn't bear the rising anxiety anymore. Telling herself she intended to make herself lunch…read her book a little to settle her restlessness…she made her way to her loft above the stables.

But the instant she reached the trees that lined the paddocks her palms started to grow moist, and Caitlyn knew she was deceiving herself.

She wanted to see that Rafaelo was okay. Except there was no sign of Rafaelo. Concerned, her steps quickened.

Surprise made her pause. Rafaelo lay on the ground. Asleep. His face shaded by a wide-brimmed hat, only the sensual curve of his mouth visible. The stallion stood beside him, front legs splayed, neck extended, deeply suspicious as he sniffed the unmoving Spaniard.

Jeans hugged Rafaelo's long legs. The khaki cotton shirt was open at his throat, revealing a wedge of smooth, tanned skin and the glisten of gold where a modest medallion lay. Her mouth went dry.

This was the man she'd been fretting about all morning?

So much for his bet that he'd have the darn horse caught and groomed by Thursday evening. To think she'd been fretting about his well-being for the past hour…how misguided could she have been!

She huffed her way into her cottage and fixed herself a BLT sandwich and wolfed it down. She was about to leave when manners got the better of her and she quickly made a sandwich for Rafaelo.

She extracted a can of soda from the fridge and placed the wrapped sandwich and drink in a cooler box. Pausing at the door, she grabbed a peach from the fruit bowl and stuffed it in the cooler, too.

The stallion was cropping the grass beside Rafaelo's ear when she reached the paddock. Despite Diablo's snorts of displeasure at her presence, Rafaelo didn't stir as she set the cooler down beside the fence post. Caitlyn waited two full minutes before it became clear that Rafaelo was not going to wake. She used the time to examine his long lean body with a frank curiosity that she would never have dared exhibit were he awake.

Finally she made her way back to the winery and tried steadfastly not to think about the virile Spaniard.

Caitlyn hurried through her afternoon tasks. She tried to tell herself that her impatience stemmed from her eagerness to see what progress he'd made with the stallion. At five o'clock she made her way to the stable block.

The first person she spotted in the yard in front of the stables was Rafaelo. Tall and powerful, the Spaniard stood in front of Diablo's stable, the bucket that usually contained Diablo's evening meal at his feet. A small amount of Diablo's dinner formed a heap on the palm that he offered to the stallion.

Diablo was having none of it.

The stallion's neck snaked from side to side and every now and then he bared his teeth threateningly at Rafaelo.

Kay, Megan and Jim were perched on the white railing opposite the stable as quiet as mice. No heads poked out of the neighbouring stalls; the rest of the horses must be eating. Caitlyn settled beside Megan.

Without gazing away from the spectacle before them, Megan said in a tone of reluctant admiration, "It's quite a battle of wills. I think he's going to be riding that horse before the end of the week."

Caitlyn shook her head. "It took Roland nearly a month to get Diablo used to him—and he had help. Jim and your dad had to hold him so that Roland could mount."

"Well, Rafaelo is the most patient man I've ever seen. He's going to wear down that horse—and without the need for extra hands." Megan turned her head. "Why are you calling the horse Diablo?"

"That's what Rafaelo calls him."

"Oh." Megan scanned her until Caitlyn felt uncomfortable and started to fidget. Finally, Megan said, "That aqua T-shirt does great things for your eyes."

"Thanks." Caitlyn's cheeks warmed. Megan had been the one who had picked it out for her.

Megan tipped her head sideways. "But there are splashes of grape must on the shirt—and on your jeans, too."

Before Caitlyn could respond, Jim said, "We were racking this afternoon. Hard, thirsty work."

"I think it's time to go shopping again." Megan had a determined gleam in her eyes.

Caitlyn detested shopping. She never knew what to choose. She was a tall, lanky beanpole and so flat-chested that she felt horribly self-conscious when the sales ladies sized her up. She was always relieved when Megan came because Megan knew exactly what worked for her—and what she would actually wear.

"Caitlyn looks fine as she is," Jim said. "Why does she need fancy clothes to work in?"

Jim was right. She had two dressy outfits in her cupboard for wine shows, the rest of her clothes where jeans and tops—most of them stained and faded. If she bought more, they'd simply end up stained and bleach-faded, too.

Megan gave Jim the evil eye. "What do you know about what clothes women need anyway?"

Jim blushed and started to stammer an apology.

Caitlyn took pity on him. "I don't need clothes."

"Let me decide that!" Megan turned her attention back to Rafaelo. "You have to feel for him. It must've been a shock to discover the old Marques wasn't his father."

"And my shock?" Kay's voice was thin. "I thought Phillip and I had something special." She broke off.

After a brittle silence, Megan said with forced cheer, "You know, he's not a bad-looking guy, my newly found brother. What do you say, Caitlyn?"

After a concerned glance at Kay, Caitlyn looked. From behind, Rafaelo's shoulders were broad, his hips and thighs lean. A horseman's build. Why hadn't she noticed that before?

"So, Caitlyn, what do you think?" Megan teased.

"What do you want me to say? That he has a very cute butt? Tight and trim in those jeans."

Jim sputtered and leapt to his feet, his face crimson. "I'm out of here." He matched his actions to his words.

Kay rose, too. "I think I'm too old for this conversation. I'd better go supervise dinner."

Megan waved off her mother. "You're excused." But her forehead creased as her mother departed. With a deep breath, she turned to Caitlyn. "C'mon, admit that he's cute."

"What about all the texting you're doing, Megan?" Caitlyn gave as good as she got, sensing Megan needed the distraction. "Is the new man a long-distance lover? Spill! Have you finally found the man of your dreams?"

"Perhaps." Megan's smile glittered. "But talking might jinx it. And stop trying to change the subject, we were talking about you. So you think Rafaelo is sexy, do you?"

Caitlyn groaned as she looked past Megan straight into a pair of amused onyx eyes. She wished with fervent longing that the concreted walkway would open up and swallow her.

"I'm flattered," Rafaelo said throatily.

"Oops." Megan gave a little laugh. "Caitlyn's indulging in girl-talk."

She was indulging in girl-talk? Caitlyn wanted to kill her bubbly friend. She couldn't for the life of her think of anything to say to Rafaelo. Her face must be on fire. What comment would salvage a situation like this?

Rafaelo saved her from a response. "Thank you for the lunch. I will give you back your cooler tomorrow."

She found herself flushing more under Megan's interested stare. The other woman mouthed, "You made him lunch?" and raised an eyebrow.

Her gaze sliding away from Megan, she said to Rafaelo, "How did you know it was me? You were sleeping."

"That's what Diablo was supposed to think." His slow smile didn't help an iota. Instead it made her remember with cheek-reddening embarrassment how she'd leaned on the fence and stared at him like some wide-eyed sex-crazed teenager.

Did he know? She rather suspected he did. With a touch of desperation, she gestured to the bucket he held. "Shouldn't you give that to Diablo?"

He shook his head. "He has a hay net for tonight—and there's plenty of grass in the paddock."

"Just none of his favourite dinner." Caitlyn felt a stab of sympathy for the stallion. It looked like Megan was right; Diablo wouldn't have a chance. "How much did the stallion take from you?"

"Two handfuls." He smiled. "But tomorrow we'll go a little further. Slowly. Step by step."

"Megan thinks you're patient. I think you're ruthless."

"He won't starve," said Rafaelo dismissively.

"I certainly hope not! Do you use the same methods with women?"

Megan gave a shriek of laughter. "Caitlyn! What a thing to ask. I've got a call to make. And I want to catch up with Mum. Talk to you tomorrow." And she flitted away leaving Caitlyn alone with Rafaelo and the provocative question that she wished she hadn't asked hanging between them.

"It depends," he drawled.

"On what?"

"It depends on the woman, her experience. If she's sophisticated, she'll have different…demands, and wouldn't require as much patience. And she'll be hungrier." His heavy-lidded gaze made Caitlyn acutely aware of tingles racing through her body. "But if she has less experience…" his voice dropped "…then she will need much gentler handling."

"Gentler handling?" Outraged and on fire with the provocative images that popped into her mind, she objected, "You can't treat a woman like you would a horse."

"A woman is nothing like a horse," he replied. "I would woo a woman with patience and care… With kisses and conversation."

"And why are you telling me this?"

His lips curved up into a sensual smile that made her shudder. "Because you are interested."

She opened and closed her mouth. Finally a strangled sound emerged. "I hope you're not basing this on what you over-heard—"

"On what? That you think I'm sexy?"

"I never said that!" She was flushing now, her pulse erratic.

His smile widened. "But you do want me to kiss you."

The sheer arrogance of the statement caused her breath to escape in a hiss. "Are you always so vain?"

"Not vain." He came closer. "I simply understand women."

Caitlyn tried to laugh, but instead of the cutting sound of disdain she'd intended, all that emerged was an airless squeak. "You really think I want you to kiss me?"

His hands came down on her shoulders. "I really do," he murmured, his smiling mouth making her pulse stop.

Caitlyn's heartbeat went into overdrive as her body connected with his. She skittered back, putting space between them until the fence rail pressed up against her bottom, preventing her from backing away. She was trapped. There was no escape. All at once her sassy confidence evaporated. This was no longer a game of flirtation. This was the real deal. The breathlessness turned to apprehension.

Rafaelo lowered his head to hers and wild unreasoning fear fluttered inside her. She was alone with him in the empty yard.

Everyone else had gone…and the terror was back.

Seven

Caitlyn tensed, expecting an assault.

But when the kiss came it was surprisingly gentle. There was no invasion, no bruising pressure to force her lips apart. Rafaelo's lips brushed hers, hesitated then brushed again.

At first she was frighteningly conscious only of how muscular he was, how big and strong. How little chance of escape—of help—there was in the deserted stable yard.

But then the warmth of his hard body seeped through the T-shirt to her body. He was warm, his flesh firm, and he smelt delicious—all male beneath the rich notes of cedar of the aftershave he wore.

She was astonished to discover that she wanted this…wanted to hold him…to kiss him. Rafaelo hadn't yet wrapped his arms around her, so the claustrophobic fear of constraint hadn't overtaken her. He touched her only with his lips. Lips that moved lightly against hers, softly, increasingly tempting.

The delicate, almost chaste kisses didn't hurt her, didn't bruise her lips nor did he make any attempt to thrust his tongue into her mouth, ram it down her throat in a disgusting parody of sex.

Inch by inch her fear started to recede.

His lips played with hers, then parted, his breath warm against her mouth. A tiny shard of anxiety splintered through her. Then he whispered Spanish words against her mouth.

A wild wave of heat flooded her, washing the anxiety away. The foreign words sounded so intimate, the movement of his mouth against her lips was endlessly tantalising. There was absolutely nothing to fear. She relaxed against him. Her arms slid up around Rafaelo's neck, and she stepped closer.

He didn't make a grab for her with rough, brutal hands. Nor did he grind his hips against her with threatening sexual purpose, his body suddenly hard and invasive. Instead he simply continued to murmur those husky, excitingly foreign words and kiss her with exquisite care.

Illumination started slowly… This wasn't about punishment. Knowledge followed in a rush—it was all about pleasure.

Only then did Caitlyn relax her full weight against the wall of his chest and start to kiss him back, their lips playing in a way that left her inexplicably aching for more.

As his fingers stroked along the sensitive skin of her inner arm her flesh rippled in reaction. Then his thumb played under the edge of the sleeve of her T-shirt before stroking down her arm again.

In the wake of his touch her skin prickled, itching for the caress to be repeated. She pressed closer. This time his fingers stroked all the way up her arm, until his hands cupped her shoulders and drew her against him.

No half expected flare of fear followed as the ridges and planes of his body fitted against hers.

Instead need rolled through her, softening her body, leaving her breathless. His hands stroked down her back in long, sure sweeps, his touch firm, confident, causing little bursts of pleasure to ignite along her nerve endings. Finally his hands came to rest at her waist.

Her lips parting, Caitlyn waited.

Again he surprised her. After a heartbeat of time, instead of devouring her mouth, the tip of his tongue slid across her bottom lip in a teasing caress that was gone before she'd realised what he was doing, leaving her craving more.

Then the taunting tip returned, outlining her upper lip, drawing patterns that brought her breath back in a rush. Hesitantly her tongue emerged to taste his. He stilled. With the barest whisper of a sigh, his tongue stroked hers.

He tasted of wood and warmth and man. Heat ignited within Caitlyn. Her nipples tightened. For the first time in years she yearned for the heady recklessness that a mouth-to-mouth kiss brought. She unwound into his body, half dreading, half revelling in the anticipated response.

Rafaelo's lean body tightened, tension singing through him, until she felt the tremors take him as he fought the urges that must be thundering through him.

She curled her hands into the thick black hair that brushed his collar, bringing his head closer, compelling him to taste her…now. Under her fingers the tendons in his neck bowed as he resisted.

His leashed restraint cost him. Against her breasts his heart raced, and she could hear the rasp of his breathing.

"*Dios.*" He lifted his head.

In a rush she became aware of her surroundings. Drawing in a deep breath, she struggled for composure and glanced around. The stable yard was thankfully still empty. Except for Breeze who watched them with curious velvet eyes over a half stable door. Caitlyn could hear the rest of the horses munching their dinner and a hoof scraped on the ground. Reluctantly she brought her attention back to the man who stood in front of her.

His eyes were on fire, his shoulders heaved as he fought to hold his breathing even. "See?" His voice was husky with the effort it took. "I will always be gentle."

Caitlyn scanned his face, her eyes appreciatively skimming the coiled muscles in his tall frame, all showing unmistakable signs of a man under tight control, the awesome patience frayed.

The skin across his cheekbones grew even tauter under her regard. "I would never—never—rush or push you into anything you didn't want."

Her gaze snapped back to his. Oh, dear heaven. Did he—could he—possibly suspect?

The kiss stayed with her all day Saturday.

So pure, so passionate. That night Caitlyn's restlessness grew as she relived it in slow-motion frames that left her melting, aching. Until flashes of other dreams—older dreams—tore into the exquisite memory, tainting Rafaelo's kiss, and wakening her to a breathless fear.

Rafaelo was not like that.

So what did he want? Why had he kissed her? Would it make a difference to how he kissed her if she told him everything? And what would be the point? She stared into the oppressing darkness.

Rafaelo, Marques de Las Carreras, wasn't staying—he'd made his intentions clear all along. Get his share of Saxon's Folly, sell it, destroy the Saxons and leave.

There was no possibility of a relationship developing between them. So what was she doing building wild hopes…impossible dreams…by fantasising about that kiss?

It was stupid!

Rafaelo and her… Why it was like fire and ice. They'd never exist together.

* * *

The impossibility of anything growing between Caitlyn and Rafaelo was underscored the next day.

Caitlyn and Megan returned from an early Sunday-morning ride, both of them breathless from the gallop they'd had along the fences at the top of the hill above the vineyards.

Despite the fact that it was barely eight o'clock, Rafaelo was already in the stable yard. He was not alone. A thickset, grey-haired man in a dark suit stood beside him.

"What's John Bartlett doing here?" Megan said as they approached, the sound of their horses' hooves crunching on the pathway.

And what was the valuator doing together with Rafaelo? The sinking sensation in Caitlyn's stomach warned her that this meeting could not bode well.

A smile lit Rafaelo's face at the sight of her as she and Megan rode into the yard.

"Hello, John. What brings you to Saxon's Folly so early?" asked Megan.

"I'm doing a valuation. I understand Mr. Carreras is a recent addition to the family."

Megan reined Breeze in. "Does my father know about this?"

But Caitlyn didn't hear the reply as she fixed Rafaelo with an accusatory stare. Instantly the warmth in the dark eyes evaporated. A cold edge of disappointment pierced her.

She'd hoped…

She'd hoped for so much. Too much. That Rafaelo would put his desire for revenge behind him once he came to know the Saxons. She'd hoped that Rafaelo could let the bitterness of the past go, that he would forgive Phillip and give up his mad notion of claiming his share of Saxon's Folly to sell it off. Clearly that wasn't going to happen.

Dismounting, Caitlyn led the mare she'd ridden into a stable and tugged the girth loose with unnecessary vigour. Rafaelo's behaviour had just brought home how much she'd been banking on him coming to terms with the Saxons. And how important the accord—and attraction—that had been growing between them had become to her.

She dumped the saddle on the stable door, taking care not to glance in Rafaelo's direction, and went to unbridle the horse.

By the time Caitlyn regained her composure sufficiently to come out of the stable, Phillip had arrived and was talking to John Bartlett while Rafaelo stood silently to one side.

Caitlyn hesitated. Then she strode forward. The Saxons were like family to her. Saxon's Folly provided more than her livelihood, it gave her a sense of community. She couldn't walk away.

Not even if it cost the fragile trust that had been budding between her and Rafaelo.

Deliberately she positioned herself beside Megan and Phillip and met Rafaelo's brooding gaze.

Nothing. She couldn't read a thing.

A sense of loss filled her.

Rafaelo looked dismissively away from her and said to the men, "I'd like to get started—the sooner we get this settled the better."

"Do Mother and Joshua know about this?" Megan still sat atop Breeze, looking stunned. "Because I didn't. Does this mean that Rafaelo really has a claim on Saxon's Folly?"

"Your mother knows why John is here." Phillip sounded weary. "Nothing has been finalised. So there is no need for you or Heath or Joshua to speculate about anything. You need to trust me on that, Megan. Rafaelo, myself, your mother and our lawyers have a meeting tomorrow morning." Phillip shot Rafaelo a hooded glance. "Rafaelo and I have a lot of talking to do."

Caitlyn's gaze clashed with the Spaniard's. Rafaelo had gone back to being one hundred percent the Spanish grandee. It was there in the implacable set to his jaw, the rigid straightness of his back and the tightness of the lips that had been so gentle against hers a couple of nights ago. How she wished he could forgive and forget.

But Rafaelo had always wanted his share in Saxon's Folly. For vengeance. From the expression on his face, there could be no other compromise. And Caitlyn knew she had little chance of stopping the inevitable.

On Monday morning, Rafaelo strode out of Phillip Saxon's office well satisfied with the way the meeting had gone. Both Rafaelo and his lawyer had decisively convinced Phillip that Rafaelo was not going away—until he gained his birthright.

Phillip had never supported Rafaelo's mother, and now he would pay, Rafaelo vowed. In blood, or rather its equivalent— in Saxon's Folly soil. The two lawyers had left ten minutes ago, Phillip's attorney promising to draft an agreement that would start the negotiation of the finer points. Rafaelo had spent the past ten minutes asking Phillip pertinent questions about the vineyard's finances. It was doing very well, and with his input it could do even better. It would be a solid investment, even though he'd always intended to sell his share….

Rafaelo didn't need to look at the man walking beside him to know that Phillip Saxon was less pleased about the outcome, or his life in general. Kay had not attended the meeting—Phillip had said that she was too busy. Rafaelo suspected she was angry and upset. But knowing that Phillip's marriage was in a state of turmoil didn't give him the satisfaction he'd expected.

Outside the winery, Caitlyn was busy hosing down the concrete under the immense stainless-steel vats. For a brief moment the tantalising memory of the kiss they'd shared on Friday evening flashed through Rafaelo's mind. But the accusation and disappointment in her eyes yesterday when she'd realised that he'd met with John Bartlett to get a valuation of Saxon's Folly overtook the softer memory.

Rafaelo paused.

"You haven't seen the whole operation yet, have you?" Phillip asked him, no doubt trying to get on his right side, before calling out to Caitlyn. "Caitlyn, will you show Rafaelo around the winery? He hasn't seen how we do things here."

"Of course I will. Where would you like to start?" Caitlyn asked as Phillip retreated. She didn't meet his eyes—and Rafaelo found that he didn't care for that at all. He'd grown used to her candour, her humour. And he'd been certain she liked him. For himself.

He shrugged. "I don't care. Just don't show me the solera where the sherry is produced."

"I won't," she assured him. In an artificially bright voice that grated, she said, "Let's start with where the destemming is done. And this is where we pour off those first premium juices." A steam of facts followed, and Rafaelo stopped studying her averted features and started to pay attention.

But he noticed that Caitlyn forgot her discomfort once she became engrossed in communicating her passion for Saxon's Folly. Her eyes sparkled as she told him her preference for French oak barrels—despite the cost—her hands gesturing to emphasise her point. Every passing moment made it clearer that if he took his birthright and sold it to cause Phillip pain, Caitlyn would suffer, too. Rafaelo frowned, uncomfortable with the discovery. He followed as she showed him where the racking was done, and led him through the winemaker's cellar where a bottle of every vintage was stored. Finally, she took him into the tasting shed. The large space was empty. The only sign of its function was the blackboard listing the wines on special, the rows of glasses on wooden counters along one side of the room and the wooden racks against the back wall filled with Saxon's Folly wines waiting to be chosen by customers.

"This is where we do the cellar door sales."

"There's no one here," said Rafaelo. "Not even staff."

"We don't open until eleven. Kay runs the cellar door sales with help from students from the local polytechnic. If it gets too busy we all chip in. It can be quite lively some weekends."

Rafaelo looked around. "Is there a restaurant, too?"

"Not yet. We have a picnic area overlooking the vineyards that's very popular. Megan has been saying we should open a café-style restaurant with a French chef and fine wine."

"That's not a bad idea."

"Roland was always dead set against it. And since his death I haven't heard Megan mention it."

"Perhaps she feels it would be disloyal," Rafaelo said, trying to imagine what he would feel in Megan's place. "Death can do that. I loved my father—adoptive father, whatever you want to call him. But we disagreed about plenty. Yet, since his death, I find myself doing things his way. Partly because I regret arguing with him about every trifle in the past, partly because it brings him back."

Caitlyn nodded. "I can understand that. We want to remember people for the good they did—the impression they made. Regret is so irreversible." She cast him a sideways glance. "You should reconsider what you are doing to Saxon's Folly—to the Saxons. They don't deserve it."

"Phillip Saxon does."

Caitlyn went silent for a moment. Then she said, "But Kay doesn't. And neither do Joshua, Heath or Megan. They're all hurting enough right now. What they need is support and sympathy—not conflict and more upheaval." She paused as Kay Saxon entered the tasting shed.

The older woman hesitated when she spotted him standing beside Caitlyn. Only for a split second, but it was enough for Rafaelo to know that Kay wished that he was anywhere but at Saxon's Folly.

He straightened his spine. The empathy that Caitlyn had

stirred in him for his father's wife should not deprive him of the right to be here. The past was not his fault. He had a stake in his future—a stake in Saxon's Folly that he intended to claim. The sooner Kay grew accustomed to the idea, the better.

But he could make it easier for her. So he smiled at her, his most charming smile. "The estate is wonderful. Caitlyn's been showing me around. It's impressive, you must love living here."

Kay's animosity receded, leaving her shame-faced. She looked away. "I always did. Saxon's Folly has the ability to wrap itself around your heart." Her voice softened.

Rafaelo felt a startling sense of connection with this cool, elegant woman who his father had married. He loved the estate where he'd grown up, too. The chalky earth was a part of him, the sap of the vines that grew overlooking the Atlantic ran in his blood.

"Saxon's Folly welcomed me, too," Caitlyn said beside him.

For an instant Rafaelo wondered if that was why she'd grown so fixated on Heath. Had she been more in love with Saxon's Folly than with the man?

Saxon's Folly was important to her. But it was important to him, too. Already his first goal was within reach: a share of Saxon's Folly. Now he needed to find out what had happened to the journals Phillip had stolen from his mother.

On Wednesday evening Caitlyn leaned against the sun-warmed stable wall and watched in disbelief as Rafaelo slipped a halter over Diablo's head and buckled it. For a moment the stallion resisted and sat back on his hocks, and Caitlyn thought he was about to erupt into a fury. Then Rafaelo walked away, unrolling the lead rope in his hand, leaving the horse nothing to pull against.

Caitlyn held her breath as the stallion's ears flickered uncertainly for a moment, then he gave a snort and the bunched muscles in his hindquarters eased. After a moment the horse started after Rafaelo. As the stallion pricked his ears, stretching his neck forward, and sniffed at Rafaelo's back, she shook her head in wonder.

Rafaelo had enchanted the damn horse.

She'd never thought it possible. And he'd done it in a day less than the terms of their bet. The certainty that he'd used some kind of horse magic solidified as Rafaelo led Diablo into his stable and, whistling tunelessly, started to brush him with long, slow strokes.

Caitlyn leaned on the door and shook her head. "I never thought I'd see this sight."

"He's a teddy bear."

"Not quite."

"Yes, he is." Rafaelo proffered the brush. "I bet you he'll let you brush him, too."

Another bet. She gave him an ironic look. "I don't think so. If you lose, I'll be flat on the straw with my head kicked in—makes me the loser, too. And it's not outside the realm of possibility. That's what he tried to do to Jim."

He'd already won the last damned bet they'd had. That she now owed him a dinner. In a fine restaurant.

A date.

She hadn't thought *that* would be possible either. Not before meeting Rafaelo.

"He won't hurt you." Rafaelo was already unbolting the door, ushering her in. "Come, let him see you, let him smell you."

His arm resting lightly on her lower back, he led her across the clean fragrant straw to the stallion's head.

"Put your hand on his muzzle."

She obeyed. It was soft as velvet. A moment later Rafaelo's hand closed over hers. "Now stroke your hand up his face, all the way to the soft bit beside his ears."

Caitlyn eyed the huge horse warily. "I thought you said he'd been hit around the head. Will he let me touch him?"

"Of course. As long as you're gentle."

Her hand moved up Diablo's nose, Rafaelo's hand over hers. Then Diablo dropped his head with a huge sigh and his eyes closed.

Caitlyn stared at the stallion's lowered head.

"He wants you to rub the base of his ears."

Diablo butted his nose against her, then lipped the T-shirt she was wearing. The disbelief intensified.

"Okay." She swallowed. "You're sure you're not a wizard?"

She felt a rumble of laughter behind her. Rafaelo moved closer, and suddenly she was aware of his bulk behind her, the powerful stallion in front of her. Yet she felt in no way threatened—not by the horse or by the man.

Brushing the horse was easy after that. There was a lazy rhythm to it and the stallion's muscles rippled under the fine ebony coat.

"I told you he'd let you brush him," Rafaelo said into her ear. "He's loving it. See how his eyes are half-closed? That's an expression of bliss."

"I can see that." Caitlyn gave a little laugh. "The terror of Saxon's Folly reduced to a teddy bear. Who'd have believed it? But I can't blame him. He's being pampered."

She started as Rafaelo's hands came down on her shoulders from behind.

"You'd like that? To be pampered?"

She gave a breathless half laugh. "Any woman would."

"You are not any woman."

Before she could ask him what he meant by that, his hands started to move, the flat palms gliding down either side of her spine.

Her breath caught. And her body tensed. Then his hands started on the return journey, his fingers kneading the muscles tightly knotted from the day's hard labour—winemaking might be art, but it could be damn hard work.

"Is that pleasant?" he asked, his accent dark and sultry.

She couldn't lie. "Yes, it is."

But it was disturbing, too—in a definitely pleasurable way. Yet beneath the frisson of delight, discomfort lurked. She stopped brushing. All of a sudden the confined space in the stable became claustrophobic.

Diablo's eyes drifted open and he nudged her, reminding her that she should be brushing him. Caitlyn drew a deep breath and forced herself to calm down.

Nothing ominous was happening. Rafaelo was still rubbing his hands up and down her back. He thought she was enjoying herself—and she was. His hands weren't staying, or doing anything inappropriate. He probably intended the back massage to relax her tense muscles.

She wanted to cry. If only she could shake the ridiculous fear that tormented her. If only that terrible night with Tommy hadn't left her stunted...

A searing, healing anger blossomed inside her. She was not going to cry. Tommy Smith was not going to paralyse the woman in her for another day. She was not going to let the past destroy whatever was happening between her and Rafaelo.

She stared at her hands automatically moving the brush over the stallion's coat. She concentrated on the rhythm of Rafaelo's hands rubbing her back, her shoulders, her nape. She forced herself to focus on the response that his hands—hands that had never hurt her—aroused in her. She forced herself to recognise that the sensations that shivered through her were linked to pleasure...not pain.

Rafaelo was not Tommy.

This was not Tommy grabbing her, tearing at her clothes. This was Rafaelo, so strong, so confident. A man who did not need to resort to force to have women falling at his feet. A shuddering sigh escaped her. His warm touch made her tingle, releasing the tension that had been building up for far too long.

The powerful, masculine hands stilled. "Are you okay?"

"I'm fine." Caitlyn started to smile. "In fact, I'm better than I've been in a very long time."

Her heart light, she turned to face him. "Thank you, that was amazing."

"You had some fearsome knots there."

"More than knots." But she didn't expand. Instead she leaned forward and placed a soft kiss on his cheek. "You're a very nice man, Rafaelo."

"Nice?" He laughed.

"Yes, nice. You're not going to ruin the Saxons, are you?"

His mouth slanted. "Why should you think that I've given up on the goal that brought me halfway across the world?"

Caitlyn paused. "You were very nice to Kay the other day." And you've been so patient, so gentle, with me.

But she left the last unsaid.

"I'm not as nice as you think." His smile held a hint of self-mockery.

"Why do you say that?"

"Diablo ate from my hand, I caught him and groomed him. Tomorrow is Thursday. And I'm not going to let you escape our bet."

Caitlyn couldn't argue with that. To be truthful she was no longer certain she even wanted to. "I'll make that reservation."

"Somewhere elegant." His eyes smouldered with some emotion she did not recognise. "I want to show you off."

Eight

"That's the one," Megan told her the next afternoon. They'd been shopping for just the right dress for hours now. Caitlyn had almost given up hope that she'd find something appropriate—something worthy of Rafaelo's desire to "show her off."

"Do you think so?" Caitlyn spun in front of the mirror. The dress fitted like it had been made for her. Flapper style, a long tube of beaded silver fabric that made her eyes sparkle. And it was comfortable. She hadn't expected that. Not from a dress. And especially not from a designer dress. When Megan had said "dress" she'd been dreading satin and taffeta, bows and ruffles.

This dress was almost plain in its sleeveless straight cut, with its scooped neckline. The glamour came from the fabric, the colour, the beads.

"There are shoes that match." Celeste, the designer, placed a pair of fabric-covered ballet-style slippers with a low heel in front of her.

More relief. She wouldn't be breaking her neck. "At least I know I'll be able to walk in those."

"And you've got to take this bag." Megan held out a tiny square that was so stylish that Caitlyn didn't dare look at the price tag.

"Done!" Caitlyn drew a deep breath and hoped she wasn't going to bitterly regret this primping.

But Megan didn't stop there. She dragged Caitlyn off to a fashionable boutique and Caitlyn found herself with two pairs of new jeans—one white and one French navy—a silk scarf top, an Indian cotton printed top in shades of melon and lime greens with white and a couple of Lycra tank tops in shades she'd never worn.

"None of these are for use in the winery while working with grape must, understand?" Megan gave her a mock frown.

"I understand," Caitlyn said meekly, her fingers lingering on the silk of the halter-necked scarf top. She bit her lip as she looked at the neckline. "I'll need to get a bra to wear under that."

"You don't need a bra under that," Megan said dismissively. "It's loose and—" She broke off.

"And I'm as flat as a board." Caitlyn knew she didn't have curves, but there was no way in hell she wasn't wearing a bra. No way would she ever again give a man an excuse to say she was asking for it. "I want a bra."

But the specialist store where Megan took her to purchase a bra was far removed from what Caitlyn had intended.

Instead of the functional—and highly invisible—underwear she'd been seeking, she was confronted by a confusing array of colours and styles. Underwear as outerwear. Pale ice-cream shades. Vivid, floral patterns. Stripes. Swirls. Dots. Black. White. Bright pink. Lace.

All of it brief and skimpy.

"Here." Megan stuffed some bits into her hand. "Have a look at these."

"These" caused Caitlyn to blanch. "Isn't there something more, um—" she cast a desperate glance around "—less revealing?" Her gaze alit on a wall of sleek underwear. "That looks more like me."

"Oh, Caitlyn! That's sports underwear. Heavy-duty gear—for marathons and the like."

"Perfect! Sounds like me. Practical." She retrieved a bra with a racing back off the wall.

"You're not wearing *that*—" Megan fixed a gimlet gaze on the beige piece of fabric in her hands "—under the silk top. Try this."

The feel of the garment Megan handed her was seductively soft. The apricot colour was feminine. Pretty. Not garish. Not tarty. Tasteful.

"Perhaps…" But she could feel herself weakening. A moment later she was in a changing cubicle stripping off her T-shirt and beige bra. By contrast the new bra felt luxurious. It was probably wildly expensive. Caitlyn glanced at the price tag and shut her eyes as she put her hands behind her and hooked up the back.

It pushed up her breasts, giving her a shape she'd never noticed having. Against the apricot satin her skin looked pale and creamy.

Feminine, she decided turning a little to the side and doing a double take as she saw the pert tilt that the bra had lent to her breasts. She cupped her breasts, the satin soft and sleek under her fingers, fascinated by the shape. For a brief flash she imagined Rafaelo's hands there in place of her own…

Her nipples pebbled under the fabric. A hot, unfamiliar sweetness pierced her.

"Caitlyn, try these." Megan's voice broke over her like a bucket of cold water.

Caitlyn ripped her hands away from her chest and felt herself flushing with guilt.

A hand appeared over the top of the changing-room door. "They're the matching panties."

She swallowed convulsively. "I don't need panties." Her voice sounded a little squeaky.

"Of course you need panties."

Caitlyn had a brief vision of the drawer back in her loft apartment stacked with beige underwear and her gaze slid guiltily back to the mirror…to the sight of her body clad in nothing but faded jeans and that exquisite bit of apricot satin that made her skin look like a pale baroque pearl.

She felt more feminine than she'd ever felt in her life. She even looked…well…sexy.

Not in a tarty way. In a natural, very classy kind of way.

Sexy.

It was a word she'd never thought of in relation to herself. Megan was stylishly sexy. Joshua's fiancée, Alyssa, was overtly sexy in a to-die-for way. She'd seen how men looked at both women—with appreciation, with narrow-eyed awareness. No one looked at her in that way.

No one except Rafaelo.

She swallowed at the unsettling memory of his dark intense gaze fixed on her. While the flashes of his uniquely exotic scent, the touch of his fingers, his lips seducing hers, all sent shivers of delight pulsing through her.

But for so long she'd gone out of her way to do whatever she could to avoid stares of masculine hunger that she'd reacted to him like a demented, hormonal adolescent who blew hot one minute and froze the next. He must think her a lunatic.

But she was no longer a teenager—which would justify some craziness—she was a twenty-eight-year-old. A woman. Caitlyn shucked off her jeans and pulled on the panties. Then she straightened to her full height and turned to face the mirror.

She looked so…naked.

Her colour high, she glanced away from the exposed plains of her pale belly, her long legs, and shivered. Then inexorably her eyes were drawn back to her reflection.

A woman's body.

The panties were cut high, higher than her own that she still wore beneath. They dipped down across her waist, below her belly button, lower than anything she'd ever worn, revealing miles of pale, tender flesh.

She shuddered. Gooseflesh rippled across her skin, caused by the odd mix of discomfort…and some secretly exciting emotion that she was too scared to name.

"Try these." Another handful of fabric appeared over the door. "For under the dress you'll be wearing to dinner."

This time the garments were silk. A silver grey that reminded Caitlyn of the moonbeams that had lit the path the night Rafaelo had walked her home. The first time he'd so nearly kissed her…before she'd panicked and ran.

Her breath caught in her throat. "Megan, I don't need—"

"Just try them." There was a hint of impatience in Megan's voice. Then it softened. "Indulge me. I don't get you to the shops nearly as often as I'd like."

It was only underwear, Caitlyn told herself. Why the hell was she getting into such a state over a few pieces of silk and lace?

Her matter-of-fact facade held for as long as it took to don the new set. She stared at her reflection. The fabric was so delicate, so fine, that her areolae were visible beneath the bra cups. Even as she watched her breasts peaked again and the centres grew tight and seemed to darken to the hue of damask rose. Beneath the panties the tawny triangle of hair created a darker shadow.

"I can't wear this set," she said hoarsely. Hell, even if Rafaelo never saw how subtly revealing the underwear beneath her flapper frock was, she'd know. She wouldn't be able to meet his eyes the whole evening without blushing. She'd be tongue-tied. Gauche and naive—a world apart from the cosmopolitan Spaniard.

Caitlyn gave a soft groan of mortification. Then she pulled herself together. "But I'll take the apricot set." She stripped off the exquisite silver-grey lingerie and tried not to regret that she didn't have the guts to wear them.

To forestall Megan from pressuring her any further, Caitlyn changed back into her serviceable cotton, emerged from the change room and said, "Maybe I should take another set in the same style as the apricot set." Moments later she'd picked out a pretty lilac set that Megan said did wonderful things for her skin.

With a last wistful glance at the silver-grey silk, Caitlyn collected the bits of lavender and apricot lingerie that she had chosen and made her way to the till.

For one crazy moment she wished she could tell Rafaelo— or even show him—the huge step she'd taken into the unknown today.

"You look lovely, *querida*." Coming from Rafaelo, the compliment sounded very different from how it had sounded spoken by Megan only an hour ago when the other woman had helped her get ready and presented her with the exquisite set of silver-grey lingerie. "Just for you," Megan had said when Caitlyn had tried to protest. Now the rough timbre of Rafaelo's voice ignited a heat deep within her.

"You look pretty good yourself."

It was an understatement. Rafaelo looked magnificent. It wasn't only the well-cut suit—Caitlyn didn't know enough about men's fashion to hazard a guess at the name of the designer, but it looked expensive. Nor was it the bright white shirt that set off his Mediterranean complexion. It was so much more than that.

The dark eyes that glinted with appreciation. The mouth that curved into a smile. The features that looked so hard until one saw the lines of humour around his eyes.

He was special. One of a kind. Caitlyn drew a deep breath. Where the hell had that thought come from?

Hastily she said, "I hope you enjoy the place I chose."

"I'm sure I will."

Ten minutes later Rafaelo pulled the BMW Z4 he'd collected from the car-rental company yesterday into a packed outdoor city car park. Alighting from the car that was a far cry from the battered wreck, he came around and held her door open.

Caitlyn emerged, straightening, and with a slight sense of shock Rafaelo looked into her eyes. He was reminded afresh that she was almost as tall as him. He wasn't used to that from the women he escorted.

"You smell nice," she said a trifle breathlessly as he lent forward to close the car door.

He laughed in surprise at the compliment and breathed in the essence of her. *Wildflowers.* "So do you."

"I'm not wearing perfume," she said sounding chagrined.

"I know. But I can smell the shampoo you used, the lavender of your soap."

She gave an embarrassed laugh. "I should have remembered. You're a winemaker after all." She stepped away from the car. "I don't normally wear perfume because it interferes with my sense of smell. And tonight I forgot."

"You don't need perfume. Your skin smells sweet and clean like the wind over a meadow of wildflowers."

He heard her breath catch as he gazed into her eyes—gleaming silver in the yellow glow of Napier's art deco streetlights.

A soft "thank you" then she was striding away, her legs long and slender and her body infinitely seductive in the silver slip of a dress that she wore.

Slowly, with a sense of foreboding, Rafaelo followed her.

* * *

All That Jazz was a shock. Instead of the upmarket café she'd expected, Caitlyn found herself in a dim cavern with smoke swirling around a small dance floor under muted lighting. While on the stage, a band of jazz musicians readied themselves to play.

Table twelve turned out to be in an alcove on a mezzanine level, giving a sense of privacy, a dangerous intimacy that shrieked seduction.

She picked up the cloth napkin, unfolded it and placed it across her lap. Her hands were trembling slightly as she stretched and took a piece of bread from the complimentary platter. The pâté knife clattered as her hands shook. Nerves. Caitlyn concentrated fiercely on spreading tapenade onto the morsel.

"Relax." Rafaelo's voice was low. "No need to be nervous."

"I'm not nervous," she said in a tight little voice. But she lied. Her insides were a bundle of writhing nerves. Caitlyn felt woefully out of her depth in these surroundings. The smart supper club. The exquisite beaded dress she wore. The man who sat across from her, his eyes hooded, unreadable.

"You have no reason to be—" Rafaelo paused and she got the impression he was choosing his words with care "—worried." He gestured around them. "We're in a public place—your choice, your territory."

She opened her mouth to correct him, to tell him he was far more at ease here in these sexy sophisticated surroundings than she. Then, remembering she was supposed to have chosen a restaurant she liked, she shut it abruptly. Well, the only advantage she possessed was—rather ironically—the fact that she'd lost the bet, so she'd be paying for dinner. She could terminate the evening at any time she chose.

There was no need to feel so shaky. She had control of the situation. Caitlyn threw him a quick look. He sat sprawled across the chair, looking relaxed and far more in command of the situation than she felt. A shivery kind of need arced through her at the sight of his hard line of his smooth-shaven jaw and the intent, snapping eyes that pinned her to her seat.

Then she forced herself to get a grip. Rafaelo was right, they were in a public place. Nothing could happen here.

Nine

"So do you come here often?" A provocative half smile curved Rafaelo's lips.

He knew! Or did he? Could he possibly suspect she'd never set a sneaker-clad foot in this venue before? The slow beat of the jazz music started up, incredibly sultry in the dim surroundings. After a moment's hesitation Caitlyn turned her hands up in supplication. "I've never been here in my life. Megan recommended it."

His smile widened, wicked with a touch of the devil. "I'm glad."

"Why?" Instantly she became defensive.

He covered her hand with his. "We'll discover it together."

Together. That silenced her. An experience that would bind them closer, increasing the intimacy she'd been trying to avoid. She stared at their joined hands, his so much more tanned than hers, the contrast marked even in this muted light. His knuckles were scarred and battered. A fighter's hands.

Caitlyn searched for a distraction.

She wrinkled her nose as she caught sight of her nails. Short, unpolished. Working hands. She curled her fingers under her palms, hiding them. No doubt the women Rafaelo dated would have beautifully manicured hands. She could imagine those pampered hands, resting on his arm, touching him. Caitlyn didn't like the sharp emotion that writhed inside her.

"Your skin is like silk," he murmured and his rugged hand stroked hers where it lay clenched on the white damask cloth.

Her pulse throbbed where her wrist lay on the table's edge. Panic began to rise within her. With great care Rafaelo lifted her hand and brushed his lips across the back.

Caitlyn froze as sensation shot through her, piercing, shockingly erotic. But before she could jerk her hand away, he'd released it. The waitress arrived with a short menu and an even shorter list of Saturday-evening specials—and after ascertaining her dislikes, Rafaelo ordered.

He handed her the wine list. "You choose."

Stuttering, her composure in pieces, Caitlyn ordered a fine red that had garnered much praise. The waitress returned after a few minutes with the wine, poured it, before disappearing again and leaving them alone.

Silence separated them.

On the stage a woman in a black-and-silver spangled dress started to sing, a throaty ballad about lonely yesterdays. Taking a sip of her wine, Caitlyn was overwhelmingly conscious of the man opposite her.

Curiosity stirred. She didn't know much about him. Only that he'd come proclaiming that he intended to hurt the family she loved. Yet, instead of cruelty, he'd revealed flashes of kindness and humour—to Diablo, to Kay and to herself—that had soothed the edges off her fears. Within her the unrelenting pressure began to ease; sensations she hadn't experienced for years were returning to life. All because of Rafaelo.

Somehow he'd taken her fear of his sheer masculine presence and managed to make her feel beautiful…sexy…qualities she'd never been aware of possessing leaving her disarmed and tongue-tied. Making a concerted effort to push the shyness aside, she set her wineglass down, flipped back her loose hair and met Rafaelo's liquid gaze. "Tell me about your home in Spain."

"Torres Carreras?" His face took on a faraway expression. "The building stands on a chalky slope overlooking the Atlantic and gets its name from two towers that were rumoured to have been built by the Moors." There was a mesmerising smoothness in his voice. "I always miss it when I am away. It is hard to believe that when I return this time, Papa will not be there to welcome me home."

"Your father, the Marques, died there?"

He nodded. "In the bed where he was born. It was in that room that I learned he'd adopted me, that Phillip Saxon was my biological father—" he glanced at her "—making me a bastard."

She flinched. "The first time we met you said Phillip was your father. I called you a liar. I owe you an apology for calling you that." Caitlyn deeply regretted the outburst. It would've hurt him. "I didn't even know you. But I couldn't believe Phillip could do such a thing to Kay."

"You were protecting the Saxons." The hard line of his mouth softened. "Your loyalty was commendable. I admire you for it."

Her breath escaped on a whisper of a sigh. He'd forgiven her more easily than she deserved. "They gave me more than a job. They gave me a home." And after Tommy's attack the Saxons had given her a sanctuary.

"That's another thing we have in common, then." Rafaelo's fingers touched her wrist, fleetingly, then lifted away to where his wineglass stood. But the brief gesture was enough to send her pulse crazy. "My stepfather gave me a home. I never realised his generosity," he continued, examining the dark red wine. "I took

Torres Carreras for granted. He made very generous provisions for my mother—and left the house and land and the rest of his estate to me."

Pretending that her awareness of him hadn't gone into over-drive, Caitlyn said, "You never suspected you were adopted?"

He took a sip of wine, set the glass down and shook his head. "Not until he told me. He thought I deserved to know the truth. And to have the opportunity to meet my own father—get to know him—before he, too, died." Rafaelo's mouth turned down. "I don't know how he could believe I would want to get to know a man who had betrayed my mother so brutally."

His unforgiving words steadied her, halting the dizzying high that filled her. "Weren't you curious about Phillip… Whether or not you had brothers or sisters?"

"Not about—" he hesitated "—Phillip, but I did wonder about brothers and sisters."

He was interrupted by the arrival of their food. Caitlyn was barely conscious of eating her meal. The crisp duck was sweet and succulent. But Caitlyn barely tasted it. She was too consumed by curiosity.

"What did your mother think about the Marques's insistence on telling you the truth?"

"She was worried I might blame her." He shook his head. "But once she'd told me about her visit to New Zealand to learn about her great-uncle, about the journals she'd discovered, I knew I had to come. One day this week I intend to retrace Fernando's steps." He cocked his head. "You may come with me if you wish."

"I'd like that." Then Caitlyn wondered if the acceptance had been wise. A whole day spent in Rafaelo's company might be more than she could survive.

The music had grown louder. The singer's voice was husky and ragged, and the sophisticated notes of the saxophone seeped into Caitlyn's soul with a poignancy that hurt.

"My mother was given the set of journals that Fernando had written by a local historical-society member… I want to find out more about those and what happened to them after they were stolen."

Caitlyn tensed. She thought of the three leather-bound journals that lay in her bedside drawer and her breath caught. *Tell him.* Yet Phillip had ordered her to keep silent; he owned them.

"My mother was delighted to have the journals, a link to her past. She hated the fact that they'd been stolen from her."

She opened her mouth to tell Rafaelo that his mother had sold that link to the past to buy a passage home. Then she closed it again. How could she contradict what his mother must've wanted him to believe? It was not for her to open more wounds. "How did your mother meet Phillip?"

Rafaelo's eyes grew hard. "The chairman of the society suggested to my mother that she contact Phillip—the Saxon family had acquired the monastery where the monks originally lived and turned it into a homestead. He thought Phillip Saxon might be able to tell my mother more about the monks who had prayed and planted vines there." His sensuous lips pursed. "He arranged to meet my mother in the town. She was bowled over from their first encounter. Naturally Saxon never told her he was married. She was eighteen…a long way from home. He hid his marital status from her. He seduced her."

"Rafaelo, did she ever tell you that he used force?" Playing with the stem of her glass, to avoid his gaze, she shifted uncomfortably in her seat. "Is that why you hate him so much?"

"No." He sounded shocked. "It wasn't rape. But he was older. Wiser. He should've known better. *Dios.* He even took her to Saxon's Folly, showed her around, raising her hopes that the attraction between them was serious, that he meant to marry her. He never breathed a word about a wife—or the child he was considering adopting."

Caitlyn thought of what Kay had told them. About her desperate desire for a baby. About how Phillip had felt neglected when she'd become lost in her world with their newly adopted baby. Her pity for Maria, Kay and Phillip grew. But it would be tactless to voice it.

Instead lifting her head she said, "Your stepfather sounds like an amazing man—to bring up another man's child as his own."

"He was." The smile that lit Rafaelo's face was full of fondness. "My mother loved him. I am certain of it. Phillip was a youthful aberration—lust."

Caitlyn nodded, noticing that he was no longer casting all the blame on Phillip. But she had no intention of entering a discussion about lust. Not with Rafaelo.

"What does your mother do now?"

"She's involved in the business—in Spain sherry is big business. It would impress her that you are a winemaker. She would like you."

Caitlyn smiled, knowing he was paying her the highest compliment he could. "I'm sure I'd like her, too."

"You should come and visit."

"Maybe, one day." She considered him, then opened up. "I've always been intrigued by the Jerez region—and the notion of producing real, authentic sherry."

She'd fantasised about going to Spain, had spoken to Phillip of taking a year off to study the methods. But after Heath had bought Chosen Valley Estate, Saxon's Folly had consumed every waking moment of her time.

Now she waited, with bated breath, for Rafaelo's volatile reaction to the sherry word. For a moment he didn't speak, and the music from the band filled the silence between them. Then he surprised her by changing the subject, and asking, "And your parents, are they winemakers, too?"

"Nothing so grand." For the first time she was glad that

Rafaelo, Marques de Las Carreras, wasn't some blue-blooded marques—even though he did bear a title. Caitlyn raised her chin. In a rush she said, "My mother was a milkmaid, my father a cattle herdsman. They had five children. I was the middle child."

He looked at her contemplatively, no hint of shock marring his handsome features. "As an only child of a very rich man, I had everything I desired. I'd imagine your upbringing was very different."

"Yes." It came out a whisper. She remembered the sleepless nights as a child when she'd vowed to herself that she would never fall into the poverty trap that snared her parents. "I was lucky—I loved school. And I realised good grades were my ticket out. Not lotto. Nor the betting on the dog racing that my father sank his weekly wages into every Friday night."

"That was wise for one so young."

"My oldest brother escaped the cycle, too. He's a property developer." Rhys was ruthless. "Between the two of us we bought my parents a smallholding. They're content." And she no longer had to worry about them.

"What about your other siblings?" Rafaelo asked.

"James is a labourer. Shannon and Rhiannon work on a sheep farm down south. Rhiannon is beautiful—she's the youngest, she's so tall, she could've been a supermodel." Caitlyn lifted her glass, the smooth wine slid down her throat, wine that neither Shannon nor Rhiannon would ever recognise. Would her naive, simple young sister have survived the cutthroat world of modelling? Perhaps not.

"Honest work. You must be proud of them."

"Of course." She blinked. Why was she telling him all this stuff? She never talked about her childhood. Too depressing. Some people even looked at her strangely—behaved a little distantly—after finding out her parents had been lowly wage-earning farm workers.

Yet Rafaelo's eyes didn't go blank, nor did his lips curl in disgust. Instead he looked interested, concerned, his gaze intense as it centred on her. "It must have taken a lot for you to get where you are today, Caitlyn."

"Hard work—and lots of determination. I spent most of my teen years with my nose stuck in school books." Later at university she'd stayed in while her mates dated and partied. She'd needed top marks to secure the scholarships that had kept her at university.

"And sacrifices, I'd imagine."

She nodded.

Rafaelo could have been reading her mind. She thought of the dates she'd missed out on. It hadn't mattered back then, she'd had her priorities—and a fat crush on Heath Saxon.

But it mattered now. Tonight she wished she had some woman-of-the-world experience to deal with a man like Rafaelo. She glanced away from him to the bandstand. The singer had moved into a lively piece and the dance floor seethed with movement.

He followed her gaze. "Would you like to dance?"

Flushing, she hesitated a beat too long. "Thank you."

Rafaelo was on his feet, helping her up, leading her down the stairs to where couples crowded onto the small dance space. Then she was in his arms, barely a respectable distance between them, blood rushing in her ears and her heart hammering in her chest.

"I have to tell you that I admire you."

There was no hint of guile in his eyes. Only admiration…and something that made adrenaline burst through her with sharp stabbing force. Unaccountably she felt herself flushing more deeply.

"I've embarrassed you," he said.

"I colour easily. It's this Celtic colouring. The one thing I got from my father."

"What about your height?"

"Both my parents are tall—and my mother is every bit as skinny as I am."

He dropped the hand that he held and rested both his hands on her hips. "Not skinny—slender."

His hand moved over the curve of her bottom and her breath died in her throat. She'd been so lost in their conversation, she'd forgotten what she was wearing. Caitlyn had a vision of the slips of mist-coloured silk beneath his hand and quivered.

Damn. She had to get a grip over her reactions. Rafaelo didn't have X-ray fingers. He'd never know what she wore beneath her finery. But sooner or later her edginess would give her away. Hell, he might even think she fancied him…that she was trying to encourage him.

That thought caused her to wiggle uncomfortably—and become even more aware of the wretched panties she was trying so hard to ignore.

Instantly his hands lifted from her bottom and came to rest very properly around her waist. But her breathing didn't return to normal.

"Relax, *querida.*"

But his deep voice, the soft words breathed into the curl of her ear had the opposite effect. Every muscle in her wayward body tightened. She tried to pull away, his hold eased, but the push of the dancers around them left her with nowhere to go.

But his gentle hold, the beat of the moody music, the singer's husky voice and the dark anonymity of the smoky club all conspired against her.

She was safe here.

Nothing could happen.

She relaxed her hands against his shoulders, and let her hips move in time to the music. Without crowding her, Rafaelo moved with her, their rhythm in tune. When had she last danced like this? Hell, when had she ever danced like this?

Lost in the unfamiliar world, she allowed herself to be caught up in the next song when it came, her body fluidly following where Rafaelo led. The floor grew more packed, the smoke machine pumped out more smoke. She edged closer to him, linking her fingers around the back of his neck, her fingertips catching in the long hair that brushed his collar.

His hair felt smooth…thicker than hers…different from anything she'd ever touched. Her fingers seemed to assume a life of their own, playing with his hair, stroking the heat of his nape.

"Caitlyn." He dipped his head, his breath hot in her ear.

Shivers of pleasure shot through her at the startling, unfamiliar sensation, and her entire body convulsed against his.

He bent his head. When his lips brushed the ridge of her naked shoulder she gave a start of surprise, her skin prickling under the flirty touch. "What are you doing?"

"Kissing you."

He spoke against her skin. His mouth opened at the side of her neck, under the secret veil of her long loose hair, and her whole body reacted.

"Rafaelo!"

He raised his head. "Too fast?"

Unable to speak, she stared at him, blinded by the violent arousal that leapt through her, unlike anything she'd ever experienced before.

"Too fast," he murmured.

Too fast? Hell! Heart hammering against her ribs, she tore out of his arms, not daring to look at the wicked mouth that had just done such seemingly innocuous, utterly erotic things to her.

"Let's sit out the next one," she suggested, staring ahead, breathless with tumult.

Back at the table she made a frantic effort to pull what was left of her composure together. When the waitress returned, Caitlyn refused dessert and coffee and asked for the bill, desperate to leave, before she disgraced herself by begging Rafaelo to dance with her and dissolved in his arms.

Out of her peripheral vision she saw Rafaelo raise his

eyebrows, but she didn't care. *She* was in control, *she* was buying dinner. If she wanted to call the evening to an end, then that was her prerogative. He didn't need to scan her with those sharp eyes— or shoot his brows to the ceiling in that superior, masculine way.

But she had no intention of meeting those perceptive eyes. Not after what had just happened on the dance floor. She'd never felt anything like that in her life, she hadn't even known such wild pleasure existed.

She was torn between fear—of the feelings he aroused in her—and a more basic apprehension that she might never feel this way again. She was tempted to snatch at what he offered.

However reckless.

Slow down, she warned herself. There was no point losing her head over this sophisticated Spaniard. No matter how compelling he was. In a few days he'd be leaving. Forever. She'd do well to remember that.

When the bill arrived in a leather folder, the waitress handed it to Rafaelo with a flirtatious smile. Caitlyn reached out to intercept it saying, "I'll take that."

But Rafaelo already had the folder in his hands and when Caitlyn grabbed the other end he didn't relinquish his hold. For several seconds they tussled, until Caitlyn snapped, "I'm supposed to pay—I lost our bet."

"I won a date."

"I don't date."

The waitresses glanced from one to the other goggle-eyed. And Caitlyn felt her colour rise. Now even the waitress was regarding her like a freak—and probably wondering what on earth a man like Rafaelo was doing with a beanpole who didn't date.

Every nerve felt on edge. She swallowed her humiliation. "Give it to me." Then tacked on a belated, "Please."

He shook his head slowly. "You paid your dues by coming on a date you didn't want."

Even less did she want to be in his debt. She cast an agonised look at the interested waitress. But she wasn't admitting that in front of a third party, so she pressed her lips into a tight line. Once Rafaelo had signed the chit and the waitress had departed, Caitlyn said, "I'd like to leave."

That was an understatement.

She *had* to leave.

The glance that Rafaelo sent her was measuring, and she knew he'd picked the coolness in her voice. But she couldn't help it. The relaxation had gone and her tension had returned a hundredfold worse than before. Then she hadn't known what she knew now. She'd been innocent. So certain she was paying, so certain she was in control.

On that dance floor she'd lost any control she had. By paying he'd taken her security. Now she was struggling out of her depth. No longer certain that she could call the shots, or had the power to end the evening.

She wanted to go home. She didn't want to risk any further unpredictable changes to the evening's schedule.

Caitlyn gathered her micro bag and was on her feet before he could draw out her chair. She exited the restaurant with Rafaelo right behind her. Caitlyn paused for a moment and drew in a breath of salty sea air filling her lungs before exhaling sharply.

"What's the matter?"

"Nothing." How could she tell him about the tightness of her skin? The frightening awareness of him that increased exponentially every time he came close? How much it terrified her?

"Do you want to walk?"

Maybe a walk would help the restlessness. Maybe a walk would prove what had happened back on that dance floor was…was a figment of her fevered imagination. She nodded jerkily, then wished she'd refused when they reached the fore-shore and found it deserted. The huge golden globe of the moon hung over the sea, and the thunder of the sea crashed in the night. A moist sea breeze caressed her arms, heightening her senses.

"Do you want my jacket?"

She was too hot, her skin felt too tight. "It's warm enough out here by the sea," she said, softening her rejection.

"It's windy."

"I'm okay." She couldn't accept his jacket, couldn't bear to be enfolded in his scent, to feel frissons of the emotions he'd awoken trembling through her. Swinging away from the sound of the surf, Caitlyn walked toward the nearest source of light, an immense art deco fountain.

"Look." She spoke as though it had always been her intention to show him the fountain. "It's lit up every night."

They stood and watched as the fountain changed colours. The stillness gave her an opportunity to regroup as they watched the greens and reds melt into one another.

"It's magical, don't you think?"

"Magical," Rafaelo agreed. But he was looking at her.

What was left of her control shredded. Helplessly Caitlyn started to tremble.

By the time Rafaelo nosed the car into the stable yard Caitlyn was a mass of shivering expectation. Did she dare allow him to kiss her? To make a little love to her? A faint doubt flared. Could she really trust him to stop if she got cold feet?

Fleetingly she considered that he would be leaving any day. *So what?* With a burst of apprehension mixed with awe she remembered the intensity of the sensations that had shaken her on the dance floor.

Could she cope with that?

Yes. She'd had enough of being a scared little mouse. She had to try start living again sometime… So why not tonight?

"We didn't have coffee at the restaurant. Come upstairs, I'll make you a cup." Her voice was high, squeaky with the enormity of what she was contemplating.

"Thanks." He gave her a slow smile that made her heart twist in her chest. "I don't think so, I should go."

Suddenly she didn't want him to go. It became vital for him to stay. Before she chickened out and never screwed up the courage to try this again. "A nightcap?"

He gave her a long, level stare. "One nightcap." His mouth twisted into a mocking line. "A sherry, perhaps."

"I don't have any." And it was a relief. She had no intention of becoming embroiled in this futile rivalry between Phillip and Rafaelo. She headed for the stairs. Over her shoulder, she offered, "I can offer you a glass of ice wine instead."

His feet sounded loud on the steel stairs behind her. "I've read about that."

Caitlyn unlocked the door and stepped inside. "Wait until you taste it."

"This is nice." Rafaelo stood in her sitting room and looked around the whitewashed walls, the wooden floor covered with scatter rugs and the exposed dark-stained ceiling beams with approval.

"It's home." Caitlyn dropped her tiny bag on the wooden chest that served as a coffee table and made for the fridge in the kitchenette, returning with a bottle of Canadian ice wine and two slender glasses. "I have great views over the vineyards in the daytime."

She poured a little wine into each glass and placed them on the chest. Gesturing to the love seat, she said, "Have a seat."

Standing, Rafaelo dwarfed the room. Caitlyn was relieved when he dropped down onto the love seat. She handed him a glass and watched him take a sip. "Deliciously sweet. Rich."

She laughed at his descriptive shorthand. "It's utterly luscious, isn't it?"

"Luscious…" He gave her a look that caused her laughter to dry up. "But not cloyingly sweet. There's no aftertaste."

Caitlyn relaxed once she realised he was talking of the wine. Plonking herself on a padded footstool, she said, "At Saxon's Folly we use chardonnay—and a small amount of pinot gris. It's freeze concentrated and while we attain a lovely fruity richness that comes from the slow, temperature-controlled fermentation, we haven't gotten near the perfection that the Canadians have achieved."

"It's not cold enough in winter here for the ripest grapes to freeze on the vines?"

Caitlyn shook her head. "Not in Hawkes Bay—down in South Island that works. It always amazes me how resilient grapes can be." For a brief moment the notion returned that she'd been every bit as frozen as those iced-up grapes. But she was finally starting to thaw.

Because of Rafaelo.

But there would be no sweetness, only bitterness. The image of the journals flashed into her mind and a hollowness rested in the pit of her stomach. Rafaelo had been so patient, so gentle with her, and she had not been very forthcoming with him.

It was time to tip the balance a little in his favour. She couldn't tell him about the journals—those belonged to Phillip, it was up to him to reveal their existence to his son—but she could share a secret side of herself.

Plucking up her courage, she said, "I told you that Heath put a good word in for me and got me a job at Saxon's Folly while I was still a student?" Rafaelo nodded, his eyes reserved. "At that stage he'd finished studying and was working at the winery. And I told you Phillip offered me job after graduation…" Her voice trailed away.

"But?" Rafaelo knew there had to be a but—it was in her tone, in the shadows in her usually crystal clear eyes.

"Something happened."

Rafaelo saw that she was struggling with whatever she wanted to tell him. He forced himself to be patient.

"There was a cellar hand who worked here." All vitality leached out her face.

Since meeting her, he'd thought Heath was the reason she froze him out. But for the first time he concluded that there was something more. Tensing, he sat up. The movement brought him closer to her. Had this man broken her heart? "*Querida*, you don't have to tell me about old flames—"

"He's *not* an old flame." She sucked in a deep, shuddering breath. "Tommy was young, good-looking—a little arrogant. He'd swagger around—most of the girls thought he was gorgeous."

Rafaelo frowned, puzzled at the distaste in her voice. This didn't sound like love. "You didn't think he was gorgeous?" He posed it as a question.

"No. Because I—" She gave him a hopeless look.

"Because you fancied Heath." A statement, flatter this time.

"Yes." She looked away. "Even though I knew there was no chance that he would ever look at me."

"Why?" His harsh question brought her startled gaze back to his face. "Why shouldn't he ever look at you?"

"Well, that's not hard." She spread her fingers. "One, I was too tall, too gangly—nothing like the petite, curvy dark-haired type of girl he always dated." She marked off another finger. "Two, my background, the chasm between us was too big to bridge."

"Because you're a labourer's daughter?" His eyes drilled into her.

"Yes, the Saxons are like local aristocracy."

"You're telling me Heath Saxon is a snob?" Rafaelo gave a snort of disgust. "That you'd fall for a man like that?"

"Perhaps I was more conscious of the differences than Heath was," she conceded.

"You were tempted to date this other man to get over Heath?"

"No! I was too involved in my work. I was painfully conscious that I had to do my best. I wanted a full-time position here as a cellar hand after I graduated from university."

Because it would keep her close to Heath Saxon? Rafaelo thrust the unwelcome thought aside.

"Even if I didn't get a job offer, I wanted a reference from Phillip Saxon."

She'd been building a career. It made sense, given what she'd revealed about her upbringing. "And?" he prompted.

"I was working late one evening. I was alone—except for Tommy. It was a hot evening. I was wearing denim cutoffs and a tank top. It was bright sunshine-yellow." Her voice cracked. "How clearly I remember that."

Rafaelo had a sudden, shattering premonition of where this was going. He reached for her hands. They were icy-cold under the touch of his fingers. "He tried—"

"To kiss me," she cut across him. "I didn't really like it. But I'd never had a boyfriend. I was twenty-three years old and my whole life had been about studying. I was curious. The next time someone talked about guys I didn't want to sit there flushing. I thought to myself that it wouldn't do any harm to let him kiss me."

"But it didn't stop there, did it?"

"No." She gave him a hunted look, her fingers biting into his. "He tried to…touch me…grab me. His hands were all over my tank top. They were grubby. It was disgusting! I wanted him to stop. He wouldn't. I struggled. He started to swear at me, made me feel dirty. The things he said." She let go of his hands and put her hands over her face, her long, elegant fingers shaking.

"Caitlyn—" Rafaelo tried to break through her distress "—he's not here now. He said those things because he was trying to bully you, intimidate you into doing what he wanted. Let them go. Don't let him keep that hold over you."

"I know that." Her fingers parted, the crystal eyes that stared through the cracks between her fingers were murky with pain. "But it wasn't just what he said. It was what he did."

Horror shook Rafaelo. "He *attacked* you?"

"Yes." It was a tiny mewing sound.

"He raped you?"

"No." She lifted her head. "Not that. He ripped my top off, tearing it. I wasn't wearing a bra. He grabbed me." Her breath came in labouring gasps. "He hurt me, hit me…tried to rip my shorts off. I started screaming." She stopped, hunching forward, her shoulders shaking.

"You don't have to tell me this."

After a moment she continued tonelessly, "I was lucky. Joshua had forgotten his house keys in the winery. He caught Tommy. He fired him on the spot. I didn't want him to tell anyone what had happened. I was too humiliated."

"So Tommy got away." Rafaelo kept his voice level by tremendous strength of will. He wanted to touch her, tell her that she was okay. But her expression warned him that now wasn't the time to reach for her.

"No, Joshua convinced me to lay charges. He was convicted—jailed for assault."

"Good!" Rafaelo tried to temper the fierce anger that surged through him. It was just as well Tommy was incarcerated, otherwise Rafaelo would have felt compelled to seek him out and teach him a lesson he would never forget.

"Despite the doctor's evidence listing my welts and bruises, in court Tommy said that I was asking for it. That I wanted it. That I led him on. *Consent,* his lawyer called it."

"He lied." Not wanting to scare her with his anger, Rafaelo deliberately kept his voice empty of the red-hot rage that burned in him against the unknown Tommy and his scumbag defence lawyer.

"And now I worry—"

"About what?"

"That a decent guy might think—"

"Might think it was your fault?" Rafaelo stared at her in disbelief, shaken by what this man…this animal had done to her.

Ten

"*Never.*" Rafaelo's eyes burned with outrage, and a muscle worked overtime in his jaw. "Any man who thinks what happened to you was your fault is not decent."

Perched on the footstool, Caitlyn stared at him through beaten eyes, her shoulders sagging at what she'd revealed. "Rationally I know all that. But sometimes I still feel…" She hesitated, not sure what he would think if she told him about the invasive demons that lived in her head.

"Guilty?"

She nodded miserably.

"Caitlyn, *querida,* you have nothing to feel guilty about." He opened his arms, and his eyes called to her to cross the small space that separated them.

She hurled herself into his arms, landing half sprawled across his chest, half on the sofa beside him. "I even feel guilty about feeling guilty," she said against the comforting wall of his chest.

"And sometimes I think that the only reason I got a full-time job here is because the Saxons feel responsible for what happened to me."

"Don't think that!" His lips brushed her ear. "They were fortunate to secure you. With your results you could have walked into a winery anywhere in the world and have been offered a position."

"Thank you," she whispered.

Above her head, he murmured, "I'm going to tighten my arms around you. I want to hold you, is that okay?"

"Yes, of course it is."

Then his arms closed around her and she felt safe. Wonderfully, heart-wrenchingly safe. She could stay here forever.

"I'm going to kiss you now."

For a moment she froze up. Then she thought about his patience, about the wonderful evening they'd shared, about how he'd stopped the moment he'd realised he was going too fast…and nodded her consent.

As his finger slid beneath her chin, she closed her eyes and lifted her face.

"*Querida,* open your eyes. I want you to see who is kissing you." His voice was so gentle that a lump formed in her throat.

Her lashes fluttered up. "Okay."

Rafaelo's head came down, his lips hovered a tiny bit above her. "Why don't you kiss me?" His eyes were warm and there was laughter in his voice. Just like that she relaxed.

It was going to be okay.

She stretched forward and placed her lips against his. He kissed her back.

The shock of it jolted her. It was unbearably sweet. He tasted of ice wine. When he lifted his head, she silently wished that he hadn't stopped. He must have seen something of her yearning in her face because he gave a little groan and lowered his head.

His lips were hungrier than before. For once the fear that had imprisoned her for so long didn't ignite and consume her. Instead curiosity stirred…and her own hunger. Tipping her head back she let her lips part.

Instantly his breath escaped in a rush and he took the kiss deeper. Briefly. Then his mouth moved to her cheeks, kissing her. Softly. Tenderly. Slowly.

Trusting him, Caitlyn moved closer, sliding her hands over his chest. Under her palms his heart gave great thumping jolts, at odds with the gentle, patient kisses he was pressing against her face.

For the first time she realised what this was costing him. He was an experienced man of the world. No doubt the women he consorted with knew the score. And yet, here he was, taking his time, content to go at her pace.

The sudden burst of affection she felt for him took Caitlyn by surprise. Not only was he awaking sensations long dormant— she *liked* him, too.

His fingers traced the scooped neckline of her dress, tickling a little. She wriggled. He moved his fingers onto the fabric. Then she stopped breathing as his hand slipped down…over the curves below. And paused. He cupped her breast and she waited, her heart thundering so loudly she was sure he must hear it.

His tongue touched her lip and she gasped. She could feel her senses sharpening, every nerve ending prickling. Every place his body touched hers—his lips, his tongue, the hand cupping her breast, the solid chest that she leaned against—all conspired to build the ache within her.

She buried against him.

"Slowly, *querida,* slowly."

After being frozen in ice for so long the return of emotion was agonizing. She felt raw and terribly uncertain, anxious, trying to second-guess what Rafaelo was thinking.

"Are you okay?" His voice was husky.

"Fine." She wished he'd stop talking and kiss her again.

His hand moved. "Still okay?"

"Yes."

"Not too fast?"

She shook her head frantically.

His thumb moved against the crest of her breast and a stab of pleasure pierced her.

The dress had ridden up. His other hand touched her leg where the dress ended. She watched his tanned hand moving against her pale bare skin, watched as it disappeared under the hemline and she began to shake.

"Anytime you say, we stop," he murmured. "You're calling the shots."

Earlier she'd thought by choosing the restaurant, paying for the meal she'd be in command of the situation. She'd been so wrong. She had no control. Her body didn't obey her anymore. It had gained a life of its own. Wild sensations tumbled through her reducing her to jelly.

His mouth was back on hers, sealing it closed. Now he was kissing her deeply, filling her, his tongue tasting her with slow, sensuous licks. His fingers inched along the soft skin of her inner thighs…higher…higher…. She gasped.

His hand stroked back toward her knee, the hand on her breast stilled, his head lifted. "I think that's enough."

No. But she didn't utter it aloud. She couldn't. She couldn't speak.

He pulled her into his arms. "Ah, *querida.*"

Hell, but she was a wimp. Why was he even still here? Any other man would have fled by now, heading for greener pastures, leaving the loony alone.

"I'm s-s-sorry," she stuttered.

His head reared up. "Sorry? Caitlyn, you have nothing to

apologise for. It is I who should apologise for taking things too far, too fast."

Too far, too fast?

Caitlyn gave a laugh that came out sounding like a sob. He'd done little more than kiss her… All very innocent between grown adults. "I'm fine. Truly."

He hugged her closer. "I won't do anything that brings you discomfort."

"I know."

That brought his head up. "You do?"

"Yes." She paused. "I trust you."

Something flared in his dark eyes—relief?—before he closed them. "I swear to you that I will never hurt you. I will never do anything you don't want to do. We will proceed at your pace. Okay?"

"Okay," she whispered. He'd convinced himself that he was taking it too fast. It was up to her to convince him otherwise.

Lying in bed, staring through the dark, Caitlyn could not believe that after their evening together Rafaelo had simply given her a chaste kiss on the cheek goodnight.

After five years in deep freeze her body had thawed out with a vengeance. She hadn't wanted Rafaelo to stop.

She would not have stopped him.

Yet he'd left.

And he'd left her wanting. Burning for him. A state that she'd never expected to find herself in.

Not in a million years. Caitlyn rolled over, restlessly pulling the covers with her and the cotton sheets were cool and smooth against her hot, aching skin. The heat that ripped her apart was a world away from the adulation she'd felt for Heath. The response Rafaelo roused in her was intense, physical, consuming.

And damn it, she liked the man, too.

For an instant she wished that he hadn't flown from across two oceans…that he wouldn't be leaving once he'd gotten what he came for.

What he came for…

His share in Saxon's Folly.

The high that she was on came to a shattering end. Suddenly she felt chilled. Dread filled her. She stared into the darkness that had turned hostile.

Rafaelo would never be able to reconcile with his father. There was too much bad feeling between them. And she was trapped in the middle: between the Saxons whom she adored— and the man she was growing to love.

Rafaelo frowned as he searched the figures working in the winery for a glimpse of strawberry-blond hair. Caitlyn was nowhere to be seen. Apart from a few fleeting encounters on Monday, he'd barely seen her since their date on Saturday night. He suspected she was avoiding him.

He eventually found her in the tasting shed helping Kay shine glasses. He paused in the vast doorway. The moment she caught sight of him a startled expression crossed her face…and something else. Something that made heat shoot to his belly.

"I'm going to spend a week with my brother in Australia. I leave tomorrow," he overheard Kay say to Caitlyn.

"Kay—" Caitlyn gestured to him.

Kay turned and caught sight of him. There was an awful silence.

"You're taking a vacation?" he asked.

"Yes," Kay said with a sigh, picking up a tasting glass and giving it a rub with a soft white cloth. Setting down the shiny vessel, she added with a hint of defiance, "Alone. Phillip won't be accompanying me. But I may stay longer."

"I'm sorry," he murmured, the words totally inadequate, but he could think of no others that would ease her pain.

Kay met his gaze. "It's not your fault."

That's what he'd told himself, too. But coming from Kay Saxon, he felt guilt eating into him.

"I should not have come."

"Of course you should have." She tossed down the white cloth. "Otherwise Joshua, Heath and Megan would never have known you exist."

"But if I had stayed away, you would not have discovered—" He broke off, not wanting to admit his father's adultery aloud.

"The truth." Kay came around the counter and patted his shoulder. "Truth is a strange thing, Rafaelo. Tamper with it and it rebounds on you. Not long ago, Phillip and I told a lie. A lie that hurt Alyssa very much. Because of a promise I'd extracted from Alyssa she couldn't tell Joshua the truth, so he believed the worst of her."

Caitlyn shifted from foot to foot, the movement drawing his gaze. Her light eyes had turned curiously opaque.

"It nearly tore them apart," Kay continued, and the brief thought that Caitlyn might be feeling guilty about some transgression faded as he focused on Kay again. "We had to confess that we had lied— to our children—and, in a different, more painful respect, to Alyssa. I have to live with it every day of my life that Phillip and I cost Alyssa the chance to develop a relationship with her brother." She drew a shuddering breath and lifted the hand from his shoulder. "I can't do that to you—or my children. You deserve to know each other."

"That's exceptionally generous," he said, not daring to admit that he'd had no interest in getting to know his siblings. He'd already been a knife's edge away from a fistfight with Heath. The place where Kay's hand had rested on his shoulder felt hollow. Rafaelo suspected he would feel marked by her generosity for a long time to come.

"It's not easy for me," she said frankly. "But it's important for you—and my children."

What she said humbled him. She could think of him in the same breath as her children, even though his existence must irk her all the time. While he'd come to spit in his father's face, claim his share of Saxon's folly and sell it. Nothing more. For the first time, he considered the wisdom of the course of revenge he'd embarked upon. Perhaps there was something in Caitlyn's advice that he needed to come to terms with the past—and forgive Phillip Saxon.

Kay was talking again. "Phillip lied to me—and to your mother. He's escaped the consequences of his behaviour for years. Your coming has made me realise that there are cracks deep within our marriage, cracks I'd pretended didn't exist—because it was easier."

"What do you mean?" Caitlyn spoke at last.

Emotion clouded Kay's eyes. "After Phillip and I married, we should have been so happy. We were young, in love, and we had a dream—to create fabulous, world-renowned wines in this corner of Hawkes Bay where we would bring up our children. But I struggled to get pregnant. Phillip went on to create the wines alone while I stewed in my unhappiness.

"My inability to conceive put pressure on our marriage. Finally, Phillip suggested we adopt a baby. At first I refused, but slowly, perhaps too slowly—" she gave Rafaelo a meaningful stare "—I came around. From the day Roland first lay in my arms, he was mine. It didn't matter that I hadn't given birth to him."

She stared into space. "Phillip said once that I had time for nothing but the baby, that I shut him out. I told him that he was being silly, that he had the vineyard. Then all of a sudden a miracle happened. I was pregnant, and I gave birth to Joshua. And then there were two babies to care for."

Her eyes were vulnerable. "Perhaps I did neglect Phillip. But I find I can't accept—"

Rafaelo had stiffened. "Me?"

Kay shook her head. "You're not the problem. It's Phillip's infidelity I can't forgive."

Caitlyn stared at Kay, shocked. "Don't do anything hasty."

"I need a little time to decide what I'm going to do." Kay gave a winsome smile. "I won't be hasty. I'll think very carefully before I start divorce proceedings."

"Oh, Kay, I can't tell you how sad this is." Caitlyn hugged Kay. "Don't stay too long in Australia."

And Rafaelo found himself murmuring the words his mother always used, words she had uttered before he left Spain. *"Vaya con Dios."* Go with God.

Kay nodded, her eyes sad. "Thank you, both." Then, forcing a smile, she said, "Now, Rafaelo, I'm sure you didn't come to the tasting shed to hear about my problems. How can we help?"

He glanced at Caitlyn and said, "Tomorrow I will be going to explore Napier and follow in Fernando's footsteps. I thought Caitlyn might like to come."

Uncertainty misted Caitlyn's eyes. "I have work to do."

Was she worried he might try to kiss her again? After her experiences at Tommy's hands he could sympathise if she had reservations. He produced his most charming smile. "I could use a guide."

Kay intervened. "I told you that you're working too hard, dear. Why, last night you worked through the night on racking wine— and with Taine sick, today's going to be equally hectic."

"It's only because the wine can't be exposed to oxygen," Caitlyn said swiftly. "Once the racking is finished, it will be better."

"All the more reason for you to take tomorrow off," said Kay with a smile.

"If I take any time off, I should use it to catch up on sleep," objected Caitlyn.

She wasn't making it easy for him, Rafaelo decided.

"You can sleep anytime. But it's not every day that you can accompany such a fascinating visitor." Kay gave him a little wink.

Rafaelo was tempted to sweep his father's wife off her feet and kiss her soundly. He'd hated Phillip for betraying his mother. Now he disliked his father for betraying this classy woman. How could one man screw up the life of two women? He gave her a broad smile in return, sensing a truce had been forged between them—no, more than a truce. A bond.

"Okay, I'll come." Caitlyn's words brought his focus back to her.

She wore her hair in a braid today, the fine mass drawn off her face to reveal elegant cheekbones and exposing her clear eyes to his gaze. Her lashes looked a little darker than normal, emphasising the stunning uniqueness of her eyes. Her mouth—usually bare of lipstick—wore a slight pale pink gloss.

Rafaelo wanted nothing more than to kiss it rosy.

But he'd promised himself that she was out of bounds. With time she might grow to love a man. But that man would not be him. It would take a lot of time—and time was one luxury he did not have. Soon he would be gone.

Emptiness filled him at the thought. He shook it off.

It would pass. Everything passed. Just as the seasons completed their cycle and the grapes flowered and were harvested, so, too, this emptiness would pass.

"Good, I'll meet you at the stable yard at ten o'clock tomorrow morning," he said, and silently renewed his resolve not to do anything that might cause her to fall apart. "And, as you're understaffed, I'm at your disposal today."

Wednesday morning dawned fresh and summery. The hot sun reflected brightly off the sea as Rafaelo and Caitlyn headed for town, the road clear of traffic ahead.

The first place Rafaelo took Caitlyn to was the historic building that stood off the foreshore where Fernando Lopez and a number of other monks had boarded on first arriving in New Zealand.

Standing outside the wooden building that had survived the

earthquake, Rafaelo stared up at the facade. "Fernando arrived after the first World War—part of a wave of immigrants who settled in New Zealand hoping for a better life. Europe was in shambles." His mouth lifted into a self-deprecating grin that made her heart leap. "You see, I did not come from a privileged background."

Caitlyn grew pensive. "You know, there's a grim irony in the fact that he came to New Zealand for a better life and died in an earthquake—while you, his great-great-nephew, were raised in Spain and became a marques in the country he had abandoned."

He shrugged. "My mother had a stroke of luck. Not many noblemen would marry their housekeeper on discovering she was pregnant."

As they walked back to the car, Caitlyn said, "He must have loved her very much for her pregnancy not to worry him."

"He never told her of his love—not for a very long time." Rafaelo paused, holding the passenger door open for her.

Their eyes held for a long, simmering instant. She was aware that Rafaelo was every bit as special as the Marques—and aware, too, that too soon he would be gone. A moment later he slid in beside her.

"He knew she'd only married him to give her baby a name. He knew she hoped Phillip Saxon would come for her." Rafaelo's mouth curled. "But of course that never happened. It was only when she gave up hope, that my father—the Marques—finally told her that he loved her."

"So when he proposed she didn't know why he wanted to marry her?"

Rafaelo shook his head. "He told her only that he needed an heir. That he was too old to find a wife. He convinced her that she was doing him a favour." Rafaelo's eyes had softened and his smile told Caitlyn how much the old man had meant to him.

"How romantic."

"My mother grew to love him. He was a true gentleman—a man of honour."

Caitlyn hesitated as the car fired up, then she drew a deep breath. "And he taught you to be a man of honour, too?"

Rafaelo inclined his head.

"Would he be proud of what you intend to do? Taking a share of a family estate and auctioning it off to a stranger?"

Rafaelo pulled out into the traffic and made his way down the Marine Parade lined with Norfolk pines. "I am not doing it for myself. I am doing it for my mother. For reparation for the humiliation she suffered at Phillip's hands." His profile was uncompromising.

"Would she want you to do that?"

He didn't answer. Silence fell between them.

Caitlyn busied herself directing Rafaelo to the site where the monks had built a smaller, modest monastery before they'd erected the magnificent building at Saxon's Folly. It had been turned into a community hall.

Rafaelo pulled over and parked in the shade of a tall hedge. Before he could open his door, Caitlyn turned to face him. "I don't believe the Marques would condone what you are doing. He told you who your father was to give you the opportunity to get to know him. He loved you, Rafaelo. He wanted to give you the chance to find your blood father…your brothers and sister. Who knows…maybe he even felt guilty for not doing it sooner and denying you the right to love your father…your birth family…for most of your life."

Rafaelo looked staggered. "No one could have been a better father."

"Perhaps he thought he was old—that he didn't run around enough with you, that he'd cheated you of growing up with your siblings."

"He couldn't think that." But Rafaelo was frowning. "No one could have hoped for a better father. You are wrong."

"Maybe." She'd said more than enough. Caitlyn opened the car door. Once out in the fresh air, she glanced curiously toward the overgrown meadows behind the building. "That must be where they planted the Cabernet Franc vines they brought with them from Spain." Descendants of those vines grew at Saxon's Folly.

"In the beginning they made red wine—for the sacrament." Rafaelo sounded preoccupied.

Unwisely Caitlyn said, "It was only later when they built Saxon's Folly that they started making fortified wines with some commercial success. Everyone knows that," she said hastily when he gave her a curious look.

"Fernando and another monk had served together in a monastery in Spain. They had experimented with making sherry years before and had learned ancient secrets passed from generation to generation of monks. They worked on perfecting what they had learned. That was the knowledge that Phillip stole from my mother."

One look at his face warned Caitlyn that now would not be a good time to defend Phillip or to question that the journals had ever been stolen. It was Phillip's word against his mother's. Instead she said, "Let's see if there's anyone here to show us around."

An hour later they drove back to Napier. They bought fish and chips and found a picnic table on the promenade overlooking the sea.

Unwrapping the food attracted raucous seagulls. Caitlyn laughed as Rafaelo leapt up waving his arms to shoo them away.

"All that land over there—" Caitlyn gestured with a sweep of her hand as he resumed his seat "—was originally all marsh. After the earthquake of nineteen thirty-one the land plates rose about two metres and the marsh drained away." She helped herself to another chip. "Not much of the city centre was left standing. When the city was rebuilt it was done in the art deco style. The most current ideas of the day were incorporated." Caitlyn nodded to a nearby building where a statue of a naked woman danced.

"Women were experiencing greater freedom and emancipation so the motif of the free new woman can be seen in plenty of places around the city." Then her cheeks reddened as she realised how pert the woman's nude breasts were, how natural her naked sensuality looked. Bowing her head, Caitlyn wished she'd kept her mouth shut and made a pretence of picking at the last of the chips. If only she could be so relaxed and at ease with her body…

"What are you thinking about?"

Caitlyn jerked her mind back to the present.

"He should've been shot," said Rafaelo grimly, guessing at her thoughts.

"He's in jail." Caitlyn didn't want to think about Tommy Smith. Not while she was savouring the last of her time with Rafaelo. "But it doesn't help to know that someday he will be back on the streets."

Rafaelo placed his hand on her thigh and Caitlyn twitched. "One day you will meet a man who will help you through this. He will be a very lucky man."

"You really think so?"

Her tone held a poignant note of hope that caused a crease to appear between his eyes.

With a nod, he said simply, "I do. I wish I could be that man."

By the time Rafaelo dropped her off, Caitlyn was pleasantly tired. To her disappointment Rafaelo made no move to kiss her. In fact, as she undressed and thought about the day, she realised he'd barely touched her—he'd made no moves at all. They'd talked. She'd discovered he had a keen interest in history and a firm commitment to family. Yet not once had he even flirted with her. Not even when she'd pointed out the flagrantly naked statue. Did he regret kissing her the other day? Had he decided she was not worth the aggravation of pursuing?

Because he was leaving?

Her heart plummeted. What had he said? She tried to recall his exact words. He'd said that any man would be lucky to have her. For a moment she grew optimistic.

Then a let-down feeling overtook her as she clambered into bed. Even if Rafaelo stayed, how could he want her while she was hiding one of the things he most wanted? Fernando's journals…

She slid into a restless sleep.

Eleven

Caitlyn came awake at the first shrill wail of the smoke alarm. Growing up on a farm meant that a healthy respect for fire was bred into her.

She sniffed. The faintest hint of acrid smoke hung in the air. Another sniff in case she was imagining it, then in one smooth movement she was out of bed. She felt for her sneakers without putting on the light. Her all-weather jacket hung on the back of her bedroom door and she pulled it over her flannel pyjamas. Before she left the bedroom, she crossed to the bedside table and quickly extracted the soft bag holding the three journals.

Out in the sitting room, the smoke alarms were deafening. She scooped her handbag off the coffee table, thankful that she was a creature of habit, and stuffed the pouch containing the journals inside. Grabbing the handset of her cordless phone, she wrenched open the door.

Stepping out onto the dark stairwell, Caitlyn paused as she caught the unearthly glow of fire.

The horses.

Already she could hear the crashing in the stables below. In minutes everything would be ablaze. Pita's shift would be finished. But where was the night guard?

Feeling for the buttons of the handset, she hit the speed dial for the homestead. Megan answered sounding half asleep.

"Megan, the stables are on fire. Check that the fire station has dispatched a truck." The smoke alarm was wired through to a call centre that should already have alerted the fire station.

Caitlyn killed the call and hurried down the last few steps. Rounding the corner, she grabbed a fire extinguisher off the wall. The flickering glow was coming from the end where the hay bales were stored. She ran down past the row of horses whickering uneasily.

One look at the flames that leapt from the bales and Caitlyn abandoned any idea of putting the blaze out with the fire extinguisher she held.

She had to get the horses out.

Caitlyn U-turned. At the first stable she reached for the halter that hung from a hook beside the door and opened the door. Breeze whinnied, a tremor of fear in the sound. Clicking reassuringly, Caitlyn secured the halter and led the mare out.

Pushing open the gate set in the fence opposite the stables, she led the mare through and loosened the halter to set her free.

Six horses to go.

A glance at the shed revealed that the flames were leaping high, fed by the dry bales.

She started to run.

Where was the damned guard? If the fire engine had been dispatched as soon as the alarm went off, it would take at least thirteen minutes to get here. A lot of burning could happen in the meantime.

She opened the second stable door.

Magic Man, Kay's dressage horse, was drenched in sweat. Caitlyn wasted valuable minutes trying to corner the frightened animal.

By the time she got the horse out, the flames had devoured the wooden beams of the hay shed and were roaring furiously.

Where was Megan? Why wasn't she—and Kay and Phillip— here yet? No, Kay was gone…to Australia. Caitlyn gave a sob of despair.

She was never going to be able to get all the horses out by herself. And once the roof caught fire…

She shuddered.

Which horse next? How could she choose which animals should live and which should die?

The crashing from the stable at the far end forced her to act. *Diablo*. Halter in hand, she ran to the stallion's stable and opened the top door. His head came bursting over the half door. She realised what the fool horse intended to do a split second before his head went up and his hooves flashed past her.

"Caitlyn, get out of the way." The shout came from behind her.

"No," she screamed, waving her arms wildly in the stallion's face to deter him from jumping the stable door and hurting himself. "Get back."

Eyes rolling white, Diablo pulled back.

Beside her Rafaelo was unbolting the door. Wrenching it open, he yelled, "Out of the way."

Caitlyn leapt sideways as a ton of enraged black horse flesh bolted past.

"There's no time to lead them out," Rafaelo shouted as Caitlyn charged toward the next stable. "Just unbolt the doors."

She glanced up. The roof above Breeze's stable was on fire. Then thankfully Megan and Phillip were there, too.

They worked swiftly, a team, opening doors getting every

horse out and when the fire engine howled through the night, Caitlyn sighed in relief.

An hour later the fire had been brought under control. The guard's unconscious body had been found beside the path behind the stables. An ambulance arrived, and the police had been summoned.

The stables were extensively damaged. Caitlyn's apartment had not caught fire but the water damage from the hoses was substantial.

"You won't be sleeping there tonight," Megan said. "You'll have to come back to the house."

"No, I can't." Caitlyn didn't want to add more strain to the situation.

"Where are you going to stay?" Megan demanded.

Caitlyn barely heard. She felt cold and suddenly shaky, despite the fact that her skin was tight and dry from the blasting heat of the fire.

"She can stay with me. The cottage has three bedrooms." The rough edge of Rafaelo's voice cut through the floating sensation.

Then she heard someone saying faintly, "I feel ill."

Hands closed around her arm—Rafaelo's hands—she recognised the strength of his hold. "You've had a scare, *querida*. You gave me quite a scare! Let's get a paramedic to check you out— I want to make sure there's no permanent damage."

A motherly female paramedic checked her out. "No burns, you were lucky. You'll be all right. A hot drink and a night's sleep and you'll feel a lot stronger in the morning."

When a pair of arms came around her, Caitlyn relaxed into Rafaelo's hold. He lifted her off the ground, whispering to her so softly that she couldn't hear a word. At once she felt safe…and secure. It was incongruous given his muscled frame and dark bullfighter looks. But she knew the gentleness—at least toward her—was real.

* * *

Rafaelo half led, half carried her to Vintner's Cottage where he was staying. Cottage was a misnomer for the three-bedroom stone house with a wide balcony on three sides. Caitlyn had been there before. As he made her comfortable on a sofa in the living room, she looked around.

Rafaelo had put his individual stamp on the place.

His leather jacket was draped over the arm of the sofa and the newspaper he'd been reading lay folded on the coffee table. The fragrance of his cologne hung in the air mingling the essence of leather, cedar wood, moss and man. Even as she inhaled the now-familiar scent, desire uncoiled within her.

She gave him a furtive look. His eyes were shuttered against her stare, but the muscle in his jaw was working. He was upset. Quickly she asked, "Which room should I use tonight?"

"I'm using that one." He pointed to the master bedroom that Caitlyn knew had a view over the vineyards to the rolling emerald hills beyond that made up The Divide.

"I need a shower." Caitlyn wasn't sure how to handle this silent, uncommunicative Rafaelo. She rose to her feet. Instantly he was at her side. "I'm fine."

He fell back. She chose the nearest bedroom and dropped her handbag—her only baggage—on the double bed before shrugging off her jacket.

Weariness swamped her and her shoulders sagged. Contrarily she wished she were back in the living room with him. Too tired even to cry she sat on the edge of the bed, her hands hanging between her knees. Her fingers were covered in dirt. Stable grime. Smudges of soot. She must smell of smoke and horse.

She definitely needed a shower. Stumbling to her feet, Caitlyn made her way to the en suite, stripped off the grimy pyjamas, turned on the faucet and stepped into the shower.

It was blissful. Minutes later, clean, warm and feeling much stronger, she wrapped herself in one of the luxurious soft bath sheets and made her way back to the bedroom. It struck her that she had a problem. She had no clothes except for the smoke-soaked pyjamas she'd dumped on the ground.

Retrieving her own clothes was not an option. The fire chief had warned that her apartment was not safe—it needed to be structurally checked before she returned. Even if her clothes survived they would be sodden.

She thought with regret of the new garments she'd purchased with Megan. They might have to be replaced. But in the meantime what was she to wear?

The towel wrapped tightly around her, Caitlyn strolled into the lounge determined to project a quiet confidence she didn't feel.

Before she could say anything, Rafaelo looked up and smiled. When he smiled like that, she forgot about her fears, she forgot about his sheer physical power, his threatening solidness. She saw only the warm eyes, the caring man who tugged at her heartstrings.

"You look like a—" he hesitated "—a waif."

With his accent for a heart-stopping moment Caitlyn thought he'd said *wife*. She stared at him with wide eyes. Emotion twisted her heart.

Waif. He thought she looked like a waif—vulnerable… forlorn…*pitiable*.

The last thing she needed was his pity. "It's this bath sheet—it's drowning me. I need some clothes."

"You can borrow my bathrobe if you want." Not waiting for an answer, he was already moving to his room.

Caitlyn waited. He returned holding a navy robe with a mono-grammed crest. "Tomorrow we'll go to town and get you some clothes, *querida*."

"Or I could borrow some from Megan in the morning," she said.

Retreating to her room for a second time, Caitlyn closed the door and dropped the bathsheet. The robe was a little big, but it would have to do. She was conscious of her naked skin beneath fabric that was imbued with his scent. It was intimate. More intimate than anything she'd ever experienced being surrounded by him, so close to her skin.

Caitlyn marched back into the sitting room to find that he was reading the paper again.

"Thank you," she said formally. "For helping with the horses, for the robe, for giving me a bed for the night."

He looked up. Instantly she reassessed. The melting heat in his onyx eyes was not that of a disinterested man. He wanted her. But he was capable of restraining himself.

And Caitlyn was no longer sure she required him to be quite so upstanding.

"Come, sit down. I poured you a glass of wine." Rafaelo indicated the chair next to the sofa on which he sat. "I've a platter of tapas in the fridge. Once we've eaten a little you can go to bed and have a good night's sleep."

Instead of taking the chair, she settled down on the sofa beside him. He turned his head, surprise in his eyes.

She felt a sweep of satisfaction. It was good to know that Rafaelo couldn't predict everything she did.

She took a sip of wine. Sauvignon blanc. Cool and citrusy with a hint of green gooseberries. *Gooseberries?*

Caitlyn held the glass up and squinted into the light. "This isn't one of ours."

"Should it be?"

"No." She flushed. "You have every right to drink what you like." Another sip. "Heath will be pleased that you're buying his wine—I'm sure he'd give you a case if he knew you were interested."

Chagrin flashed in his eyes. Caitlyn grinned inwardly. It was good to catch him off balance for a change.

"I wouldn't ask—I simply wanted to check out the competition."

"Competition?" She stared at him. "Heath isn't competition. He's your brother."

"Half brother," he growled. "With none of the closeness from growing up together that the word *brother* suggests. We are strangers to each other."

"But it needn't remain that way. Don't you see? This is what your father—the Marques—wanted. He wanted you to have the chance to get to know your family."

"I have a family. I don't need—"

"You have a mother. That's all." She glared at him in frustration. "Here's the chance to have so much more. Brothers. A sister. Even a birth father."

"Phillip only supplied the seed for my existence."

Caitlyn shook her head. But at least he wasn't rejecting the brothers and sister quite to the same extent as Phillip. Perhaps there was still a chance. But she'd flogged this horse to death, now was not the time to say more.

"Nothing to say?"

She remained silent.

"Sulking?"

That got to her. "I never sulk. All I can say is that I grew up in a large family and I wouldn't give up any of my brothers and sisters. Sure, we've squabbled over the years, but I love them. Think about that, Rafaelo, before you wrest a share in Saxon's Folly and auction it off. Think about the love that you might be shutting out your life."

"Quiet! I don't need a lecture. The only kind of love I care about is this kind." Before she could object he'd swept her onto his lap and he was kissing her.

She knew that he'd intended to shut her up. She was furious with him for choosing this tactic…and with herself for caring. But she loved him and she loved the Saxons. It was a hopeless situation. Yet she couldn't stop what she felt. The emotional connection had grown stronger with every passing day. She loved him.

So she kissed Rafaelo back with all the pent-up longing that had been building up for days. He tensed as her fingers locked behind his neck and pulled his head down to her. Then he exhaled and she knew she'd won.

She was not going to make this easy for him. She was not going to let him do what he'd come to do and walk away unscathed…and forget all about her.

He'd learn to care. *He had to.* Because she already cared far too much.

The robe parted. She heard his shocked exhalation as it gaped open, baring her body for his inspection. For one wild moment his eyes took in the full creamy mounds, the stiff dusky-pink tips, then he swore and flung himself away from her.

"Forgive me, Caitlyn, I never intended for this to happen."

Twelve

"Don't go."

Rafaelo halted. Caitlyn was staring at him with an expression that on another woman's face he might have described as hunger.

But never on Caitlyn's.

She'd fought a fire. Her home was water-logged. Her personal belongings drenched by the fire hoses. Her most treasured possessions possibly destroyed. She must be feeling desperately vulnerable, seeking reassurance.

To imagine she wanted him would be crazy—a sign that he'd lost his reason. Although he nearly had when he'd seen the fire at the stables. The idea of anything happening to Caitlyn—

He refused to think about it.

"Do you want a cup of tea?" That might soothe her and help her sleep. He needed a stiff drink.

"I still have some more wine." She raised her glass and he watched with a frown as she took another sip. The eyes that peered over the glass at him were bright and defiant. "I don't want you to stop."

Maybe she was tipsy. He could understand her not wanting him to leave...but to want him to keep kissing her? That had to be the wine talking.

"*Querida,* if I kiss you again, I might never be able to stop." Under the circumstances Rafaelo was proud of the patient tone he managed.

"You'd stop if I asked."

He would? There was such blind trust in her statement that Rafaelo's chest tightened. He quaked at the thought of drawing back once he'd tasted her...

Her trust was important. Taking a deep breath, he said. "Yes, I would."

She patted the cushion beside her. "Then come here."

He sank down beside her, his gut churning with a mix of desire and concern and a feeling that he was taking the most dangerous risk of his life.

As he lowered his head she said, "I want more than kisses, Rafaelo."

"What?" Shocked by her primal throaty tone, his every sense on red alert, he reared back.

"I want everything...everything I've been missing for my whole adult life."

"Caitlyn." He sucked in a shuddering breath. "Let's take it slowly, there's no hurry."

"No! I don't want to wait any longer. You'll be leaving soon. I could've died tonight. I didn't. I'm fine. But it could have happened. Tomorrow I could be killed in a car accident—like Roland Saxon was. I've spent years trapped in the past. I don't want to live like that anymore. I want to be free."

Mierda. He tried to clear his head. He didn't need to be reminded that he might have lost her. He'd been trying not to think about that. Nor did he want to think about why a world without Caitlyn would be as empty as a world without joy. "What you're feeling is a normal reaction to a traumatic event. You'll feel different in the morning, believe me."

"I won't. I want you."

She'd hate him tomorrow if he did what she asked. And she'd detest him when he left for Spain without her. Though the thought of that was becoming harder and harder to accept. He couldn't make love to her; he had to protect her from herself. "You don't want me. All you want—" He stopped midsentence. She'd pushed the robe off her arms and now reclined naked in front of him.

He blinked furiously.

"Do you believe me now?"

"Caitlyn!" Her skin looked as soft and luscious as a ripe peach and her hair spilled over delicate pale shoulders presenting a vision so excitingly sensual that he swallowed hard and closed his eyes to shut out the blatant temptation she offered.

"Don't you want me?"

His eyes snapped open. "Not want you? Don't be an idiot." He took in the uncertainty in her eyes, the hectic flush that lay across her cheeks. She was embarrassed. Uncomfortable. She imagined he was rejecting her because he didn't desire her. *Idiota.* "Of course I want you. But I am trying very hard to be noble—to do something that's in your best interests."

"*My* best interests?"

Her disbelief stung. "Look—" he pointed to his groin and said brutally "—does that look like I don't want you?"

She glanced to where his black pants revealed the thick ridge of his erection. Her breath snagged with an audible gasp. Instantly Rafaelo felt his flesh surge as she lifted wide eyes to his. Yet instead of apprehension, the eyes that met his glowed with anticipation.

"Caitlyn," he said hoarsely, "you are making this very difficult."

"I want to make it impossible." She leaned over him, her long silky hair brushing his face. No hint of smoke lingered. She smelled of fresh shampoo and wildflowers.

So tempting.

Too damned tempting.

"I want it to be you." Her eyes, so clear and bright with emotion, blinded him. "I know that you will be gentle…and patient."

Madre de Dios. He shook his head—a last-ditch effort to deter her. "You can't know that."

"I do know," she insisted. "You were patient with Diablo—"

He swore softly, in Spanish. "Diablo is a horse. That is no recommendation." Then he suppressed the insane urge to laugh. Never had a woman asked him to make love to her on the basis of his skill with a horse. Usually it was because of his family name, his connections, his wealth. His eligibility.

Only Caitlyn didn't care about the things that every other woman wanted. Only Caitlyn touched his heart with her candour, her honesty. When…how…had she become his whole world?

She was speaking, he jerked his attention back to her. "The day you convinced me to stroke Diablo, with your hand over mine, you said someone had hit him around the head. You crooned to him so gently. It reminded me of something. The way you comforted me when I was afraid. I trust you, Rafaelo. I know you would never hurt me."

Why the devil was he arguing? He wanted her with a hunger that was foreign to him. "If you're determined to do this, then I suggest we retreat to the bedroom."

Apprehension clouded her eyes. Then she said, "Okay."

He'd fully expected her to chicken out—to tell him that she'd made a mistake—when he rose to his feet and made for his bedroom. But she was incredibly brave. Foolishly so. She followed him, catching his fingers and threading them between hers. He could hear her shaky breathing, and her fingers trembled under his. In the master bedroom, he sat down on the king-sized bed so as not to loom over her.

She hovered in front of him, his robe gaping open in the front. For a moment he thought she might have had second thoughts and he groaned inwardly. He forced himself to keep his gaze on her face, not to peek at the bare skin that he craved another glimpse of. She was so lovely, so incredibly gallant.

Suddenly he didn't want her to be sensible, to back out.

Surrendering her fingers, he put his wrists together and stretched them toward her. "Tie my hands if it makes you feel easier."

Shock glinted in her eyes. *"Tie your hands?"*

"You might feel safer."

He watched as her throat bobbed. But something gleamed in her eyes. Curiosity? Excitement?

"Look in the cupboard—there are ties and belts that you could use." He gave her a ghost of a smile, even though he'd never felt less like laughing in his life. *Dios,* he hoped she was going to change her mind. This couldn't be easy for her. He wouldn't blame her if she decided to cut and run.

"But you'd still have your feet free," she pointed out.

"Tie those, too—if you want."

She stared at him, clearly shocked. "You'd surrender that much control?"

"Lovemaking isn't about control. It's about pleasure." He gave her an oh-so-slow smile, doing his best to banish her fears.

"You… You are incredible, Rafaelo."

"No, *querida,* you are."

"Why didn't I meet you before…?"

The despair in her eyes tore at his heart. "*Querida,* I can't erase what happened in the past. But I can show you that not all men get their kicks out of fear and pain. I can promise you a night of pleasure…and passion."

She stared at him, and he could see that she was incredibly tempted. "Nothing bad really happened. I wasn't raped. I was attacked…and touched." She shuddered.

He didn't reach for her, but intense emotion burned in his chest. "Don't *ever* let me get my hands on him."

She gave a half sob, half laugh. "Joshua dealt with him. I don't know what he said to…him…before he fired him."

"Come here."

She perched on the bed beside him, a little stiff. Gently Rafaelo wrapped an arm around her, and tucked her under his shoulder. He rested his head against her hair, willing her to understand that he would never harm her.

"I don't need your hands tied," she said. "I don't fear them, I know that they will give me pleasure—not pain." She raised her head and smiled at him. It was like seeing the rainbow come out after the storm. "One day we can play those games, for fun. Tonight I want you to touch me—"

Rafaelo growled, his restraint breaking. "Oh, *querida,* I will certainly touch you…and taste you…and adore every inch of you."

Her heart leapt. And for once the fear remained absent.

Shrugging off his shirt, Rafaelo lay back on the bed. "Come here," he murmured huskily, pulling her on top of him.

At first the position felt precarious, being perched on top of him, but then as the heat of his torso penetrated the thin robe she wore, Caitlyn began to feel the hot stirring of desire. Bending her head, her hair spilling around his face, she placed her mouth against his, and his lips parted.

He tasted wonderfully familiar. The feelings that his kiss aroused started gently, seeping through Caitlyn in sensuous layers until her skin was warm and tingles started to whisper down her spine.

When his hands slipped under the robe, the warmth ignited into a hot glow. Caitlyn shivered with wakening desire as the robe slid down over her shoulders, his fingers smoothing over her skin…around her ribcage…across the sensitive skin of her neck.

She groaned against his mouth as he touched her and arched upward when his fingers found her nipples. Heat sliced through her, and her eyes closed.

Caitlyn's whole being was focused on his touch, on the delicious feelings he aroused within her. His fingers moved, caressing, playing with the pebbles of flesh. At last his hands moved away, and she moaned in disappointment as he braced them against her and moved her away from his torso.

Opening her eyes, she looked into molten dark ones.

Then he pulled her down. At the very last instant she realised what he was going to do. A wild moan broke from her as his mouth closed on the tip of her breast. A streak of fiery heat tore through her and gathered low in her belly and she shuddered, focusing fiercely on the unexpected dark delight that splintered through her.

Caitlyn didn't even notice when he finally stripped off the robe. It was no big deal to be naked against him, not when his mouth had tasted her, brought her so much pleasure.

His hands stroked her all over. Long, sweeping movements that left heat and fire in their wake. Caitlyn's whole body burned. When his hand slipped between her thighs, the temperature went up another notch, and her pulse hammered in her throat.

His fingers moved deftly and her breath caught at the sensation that ripped through her. "Oh, Rafaelo."

The smile he gave her was slow and knowing. "Take your time. Enjoy."

Her hips lifted higher as his fingers edged deeper. Her breath ragged, her pulse wild. "Stop," she demanded. "Or there'll be nothing left."

"Then we can start again." The promise in the eyes below hers made heat rush through her.

"It's hardly fair, you're wearing too many clothes," she

murmured when she realised she wore not a stitch, while he still wore pants.

"Are you sure?" He gazed up at her through heavy-lidded eyes.

A surge of emotion shook her. She loved him so much. "Very sure."

"You don't want to stop?"

She groaned. "No! It's not too far…nor too fast."

"Just making sure." He was smiling up at her, his full, passionate lips curving with amusement, the small white scar below giving him a wicked look that made her go weak with desire.

"Are you laughing at me?" she asked softly.

"I wouldn't dare," he said with a grin.

Caitlyn shifted. There was the sound of a zip rasping. His smile vanished. She moved, just enough to make him groan, then she pushed the black pants and his underwear away.

"Good," she purred. "I'm very pleased to hear that."

There was shock in his eyes—and something else. "Caitlyn—"

"Don't say a word." Legs either side of his hips, she shifted again. "Not a word."

The hard length of his erection surged against her softness. But he remained silent, except for the whisper of a groan as she tantalised him, riding him delicately.

By the time he slid into her, Caitlyn was moaning. There was a moment of resistance, Rafaelo gasped, stilled, then his arms pulled her close.

"That was not funny," he muttered. "But I am inordinately pleased."

And as his hands stroked her back in long deliberate sweeps, his hardness claimed her until Caitlyn felt herself shimmering, hanging on a thread, until she started to tremble. The thread snapped and she fell into an abyss of pleasure.

And Rafaelo's body shivered against hers as the pleasure shook them both.

* * *

"Will you marry me?"

Rolling away from the heat of Rafaelo's body, Caitlyn pulled the robe off the bottom of the bed and tucked it firmly under her arms. Decently covered, she felt safe enough to sit up. *"What?"*

"Will you marry me?" he repeated.

He lay on his back, staring up at the ceiling, his hands fisted by his sides.

This was so tempting…she *did* want to marry him.

But it wasn't sensible.

"It's not practical for me to marry you," she explained. "If I married you I would need to leave my work—which I love—and all the people who are very close to me."

A strange expression shadowed the face that had become so precious to her. "They're not even your family."

"The Saxons are as close as my family." Caitlyn watched as his brows lowered ominously.

"But you would be with me," he objected with a hint of his old arrogance. "I would be your family."

If he loved her that would be enough. But he didn't…

And even if he had loved her, once he discovered that she'd had the journals he'd sought all along, that she'd been a vital part of the success of Saxon's Folly's sherry-style fortified wines, that would all go up in smoke. She sighed. Better she end this discussion before it all became too painful.

Caitlyn shook her head. "No, Rafaelo, there's no point in this discussion." She slid her legs off the bed and got to her feet, clutching the robe around her.

"Where are you going?"

"I'll be back in a moment." She went to the bedroom where she'd showered and retrieved her handbag. For a long moment she hesitated. Then she spun around and made her way back to his bedroom, still clad in the soft robe.

She extracted the pouch out of her bag and threw it on the bed. "This is what you want."

He made no move to touch it. "What is it?"

"Open it."

Not taking his eyes off her, he sat up and reached for it. Caitlyn stood beside the bed and did her best not to stare. He made no effort to hide his very blatant, very male nudity. The journals fell onto the bedcover beside him. His gaze dropped and his expression changed. He knew what he was looking at. "Why do you have these?"

She didn't answer.

He flipped the cover open. "They're written in Spanish." He looked up, surprise in his eyes. "My mother never mentioned that. You speak Spanish…" His voice trailed away.

She nodded.

"It wasn't Phillip…it was you."

Caitlyn knew she'd never forget the expression in his eyes for as long as she lived.

"It was you who read them, you who studied Fernando's methods and applied them."

"Yes." She didn't lie. Nor did she apologise. It was way too late for that.

He pushed himself up and sat on the edge of the bed, raking his fingers through his hair. Stretching, he reached for his pants where they lay in a heap on the floor and pulled them on, before rising to his feet. Caitlyn felt the distance between them widening.

"Why didn't you tell me?" he asked, his eyes drilling into hers.

"At first I didn't realise how important it was to you. By the time I did, I knew you hated the Saxons—hated Phillip. That more than anything in the world you wanted to hurt him. I couldn't let that happen."

He stood in middle of the room, facing her. No hint of the lover remained. "He still stole them from my mother."

She could no longer let Phillip bear the full weight of his blame. "He didn't steal them—he bought them from your mother."

He lifted his head, giving her that Spanish grandee glare. It was as intimidating as ever. Then he said, "That's not true!"

She gave him a sad smile. "Are you saying that I'm lying?"

For a timeless moment the memory of their first meeting lay between them.

"No, I'm not calling you a liar," he said, his voice ragged. "There must be some other explanation. You must have been told a lie."

"There isn't another explanation, Rafaelo." Caitlyn's heart ached for him. She wanted to go to him, put her arms around him, tell him she loved him. But she couldn't. "Your mother sold them to Phillip. They sat in Phillip's office for nearly three decades. It wasn't until I read them that he realised exactly what was in them. He had some vague idea—Maria had shared some snippets. And he'd had a Spanish interpreter look at them, but she wasn't a winemaker and couldn't understand the nuances."

"You always said that you were fascinated by sherry."

Caitlyn didn't make excuses for herself. "And this was my way to make my mark in the industry. The girl from nowhere…to the chief winemaker of one of the most prestigious estates in Hawkes Bay." With every word the distance between them yawned wider.

To his credit, his expression didn't change. No sneer marred his near-perfect features. "I can understand that you were ambitious. The journals would have been a godsend to you, to help you establish the reputation you craved."

It sounded so cold, so ugly.

Caitlyn glanced away. "I'm sorry."

"The day I said that I wanted my share…that I intended to auction it…"

"Yes."

"Why didn't you speak up then?"

"I started to. But Phillip gave me a look that warned me to stay silent. Later he told me that he'd bought them from your mother. That telling you I had them would only lead to more problems. He feared you might not believe him—and lay charges of theft causing more scandal when Kay was already fragile. Or you might be angry that your mother had sold them." She drew a shuddering breath. "I didn't know what to do. I was torn apart."

There was a hint of softening in his gaze. Small, but it was there. "You've been caught between the devil and the dark blue sea."

"An impossible place." She hunched her shoulders. "But you wanted vengeance, to hurt the Saxons by claiming a share of Saxon's Folly and selling it—that made it easier to view you as the villain of the piece." Until he'd shown her the patient, gentle side of himself. Then she'd been lost.

Rafaelo sighed, a harsh sound. He raked a careless hand through the long black hair that she knew felt like rough silk. "So what happens now?"

There was a long silence. Caitlyn tensed. She couldn't bear to think about it. Their lovemaking had brought such exquisite joy. But now that feeling of oneness was gone, leaving her feeling drained. And empty. "I don't know. I suppose you go home."

He gave her a long, unreadable look. At last, his jaw set, he said, "I still want to marry you."

Hope flickered inside her. Could he possibly feel for her what she felt for him? "Why?"

After a long silence, during which Caitlyn's heart sank to her toes, she knew she had been right to refuse his chivalrous offer—however much she'd wanted to accept, he finally said, "I'm not sure where this desire comes from. I did not come to New Zealand to seek a wife."

She drew herself up to her full height, making every inch count. "No, you came seeking vengeance…and the journals."

His fingers attacked his hair again, pushing it back off his face.

"Maybe. That's why you won't marry me. Because by marrying me you think you would be betraying your beloved Saxon family."

Caitlyn took a risk. "I don't believe you would harm any of them." She stared at him boldly, holding her breath. "Given the care you took of Diablo, your gentleness with me, I don't think you could ever take something that means the world to the Saxons and auction it off to the highest bidder for cold hard cash."

His jaw clenched more tightly. "I could."

"But you won't. You wouldn't hurt Kay—or Megan or Joshua or Heath—because of Phillip's sins."

He gave her a calculating look. "Not if you marry me."

"Oh, no." Caitlyn shook her head so hard that her hair whipped around her face. "You're not blackmailing me. You don't even possess that share yet. And even if you did, I don't come with that kind of price on my head. There's only one reason I'd marry a man."

"What's that?"

"Love," she said quietly. "Not obligation, not barter for my virginity, not blackmail. Only love."

He frowned at her for a long moment. Then he turned away. "Then you are correct. There is no point discussing this further."

There had been frustration…and anger…in that look. But the rigid line of the naked back he presented to her, made it clear that there was no future for them.

Caitlyn couldn't help thinking that he must hate her. Especially when she saw he'd taken the journals with him.

Thirteen

Caitlyn's eyes were scratchy and bone-dry from lack of sleep. Last night, despite her exhaustion, she'd hightailed it from the Vintner's Cottage clad only in Rafaelo's robe. She'd been welcomed at the main house without any questions.

This morning she'd borrowed a T-shirt and a pair of too-short tracksuit bottoms belonging to Megan to wear to work—while Phillip insisted she take the day off—and give herself a chance to recover.

After lunch, Megan whipped her into Napier to buy some jeans and shirts, underwear and shoes. Caitlyn was grimly amused by the thought that after years of no shopping, suddenly it seemed she was doing little else. But when they arrived back at Saxon's Folly, her amusement dried up.

Rafaelo paced the forecourt waiting for her.

"I came by to see how you are." His eyes searched her, his inspection telling her more than words that he'd been worried. He must care. A melting sensation filled her, which she immediately suppressed.

He didn't love her, she told herself fiercely.

But before they could have the discussion he clearly wanted, a police car cruised slowly down the lane. Two police officers wearing stiff uniforms and sombre expressions stepped out and slammed the doors in unison.

"Caitlyn Ross?" asked the taller of the two.

She nodded.

"Is there somewhere we can talk?"

She took them to the winery, into the small cubicle packed with books and magazines and racks of wine that served as her office. It was with little surprise that she realised Rafaelo had come, too. He stood just inside the door, tall, dark, his eyes very fierce and his stance protective.

"We'd like to talk to Ms. Ross alone." The older cop was solid, with grey hair and a worn expression where life had lined his face with harsh experience.

"I don't think so." Rafaelo looked formidable. "Unless you'd rather make an appointment to meet her with her attorney present?"

"Ms. Ross doesn't need an attorney right now. We simply want a statement." The taller, younger cop's tone grew conciliatory as he eyed Rafaelo up and down.

Rafaelo stayed.

"Do you have any enemies, Ms. Ross?" The older of the two asked her after she and the cops had taken the only three chairs. Rafaelo loomed in the doorway, like a dark angel.

Distracted, Caitlyn shook her head. "Why?"

The older policeman spoke, "There are signs that last night's fire was no accident."

"You're saying it was deliberate?" She searched the front of his uniform for a tag. "But why, Constable West?"

"It's sergeant." He waved away her apology. "That's what we'd like to find out. You live above the stables, correct?"

She nodded again.

A horrible thought struck her. "What about the guard? Does this mean that it wasn't a piece of timber that struck him? That he was deliberately injured?"

"We can't say yet, ma'am. There's a lot of work to be done."

"Do you have any suspects yet?" Rafaelo asked. The older cop gave him a measuring glance, but neither answered him.

"What about ex-boyfriends who you parted with badly?" asked the younger cop.

"No one springs to mind."

"Anyone who rides a black motorcycle?"

She started to shake her head, then stopped. A black motorcycle…

Could there be a connection?

"There was a black motorcycle in the paddock several weeks ago. It scared the stallion, causing Alyssa to fall off the horse she was riding."

Neither cop looked surprised. Another note was made. Caitlyn had a feeling she wasn't telling them anything they didn't already know.

"Tell them about Tommy."

"Tommy Smith?"

Her heart started to thud at the cop's sudden expression of interest. Her gaze slid to Rafaelo. "But he's in jail."

"Tell them."

She did, hating every moment. But it was strangely cathartic. She hardly ever talked about Tommy's attack on her, she realised.

The grey-haired cop took copious notes. When he'd finished, he asked Caitlyn a few more questions, then they packed up their notepads and left.

Caitlyn turned to Rafaelo. "If the fire was started deliberately, I certainly hope they catch whoever did it."

Rafaelo drew her close. "When I think what might have happened…" A shudder shook his big frame.

Rafaelo walked into the homestead that evening, Caitlyn by his side, with the deliberate tread of a man with a mission.

Time was growing short. He didn't have much more time in New Zealand, Torres Carreras was waiting, and he'd stayed longer than he'd intended. But he had a lot to accomplish in the short time he had left. His hand tightened around Caitlyn's waist and he led her to where Phillip stood in a group with his sons— his legitimate sons.

For the first time Rafaelo felt no resentment. After setting the parcel he carried under his arm on a conveniently located side table, he nodded to Joshua and Heath. Both men stepped forward, their faces alight with welcome.

"Caitlyn, I've got a glass of pinot gris for you. What would you like, Rafaelo?" Joshua asked.

Rafaelo blinked.

The feeling of having walked into another world—a world filled with warmth and approval and acceptance—grew as Heath chatted to him about harvests, about rain, with no hint of animosity. But when Phillip turned to smile at him, Rafaelo knew something was wrong.

"What's happened?" he asked, suspiciously.

"We want to thank you for what you did."

"What I did?"

"For rescuing Caitlyn." Megan hugged him. "She's part of our family."

Rafaelo tried to relax.

"I can never thank you enough," said Phillip.

Rafaelo looked around the circle. All of them were smiling. They loved Caitlyn. She belonged here. How could he ever uproot her from the people who were her family, the place that was her home? He glanced at her. She was smiling, too, the translucent eyes smoky with an emotion that made his throat close.

She was smiling at him.

Finally he said, "She was doing fine by herself, she would've been all right."

"I couldn't stop wishing the cavalry would arrive," she said, contradicting him, her eyes still filled with that softness that he decided must be gratitude.

Ivy, the housekeeper, called them to the dining room and the meal passed in noisy conversation. Amy Wright arrived a little late. Rafaelo had seen her in the winery, her head bent over the computer, but he'd never really spoken to her. She was small and fine-boned with a dark bob and stricken eyes. Tonight she greeted him with a smile before Megan bore down on her.

Looking up he saw that Caitlyn was still smiling at him. He gave her a searing look that warned her that if she continued there would be consequences.

The smile turned wicked.

Rafaelo knew it was going to be a long dinner.

After dessert had been served they adjourned to the seating area in the salon. Phillip served chilled *Flores Finos* in small glasses. Rafaelo couldn't bring himself to refuse. He sat beside Caitlyn on one of the sofas and the award-winning fortified wine lingered on his tongue, the taste unique.

Phillip clapped his hands and everyone fell silent. "I have a gift I'd like to present to Rafaelo."

Rafaelo rose to his feet and picked up the parcel he'd set down on one of the side tables when he'd come in. "I have something for you, too. This is not a gift—it belongs to you." He'd read the diaries last night, savouring his great-great-uncle's words. It had given him great pleasure. "I understand from my mother that you bought them from her."

"Your mother?" The whisper came from Caitlyn.

He glanced at her and nodded. "I called her this evening, just before dinner. I wanted to let her know that I had a few matters to tie up here before I could come home. I asked her. She told me that she needed the money. You told me the truth." He tried to convey his appreciation to Caitlyn. But it was impossible for her to know what it meant to him. He turned back to Phillip. "The journals are yours."

"No." Phillip Saxon shook his head. "Fernando was your blood relative. The secrets in there belong to you. Those are yours to keep, my son."

My son. The words caused a floodgate to open in Rafaelo's chest. He felt relief, wonder…and deep down in the farthest reaches of his heart the first stirrings of affection for the man who stood in front of him, his blood father.

"Thank you." Rafaelo hesitated. "This is difficult for me, and I fear I am not yet ready…but I would like in time to call you 'father' if I may?"

The sheen of tears filled Phillip's eyes. He stepped forward and hugged Rafaelo.

For a moment Rafaelo froze, then he clasped Phillip's upper arms. Over Phillip's shoulder Rafaelo read the relief that spread across Caitlyn's face. It made him feel humble. This was her doing. She had brought him to a point where he could accept Phillip as his father.

Stepping back, Rafaelo said huskily, "You could not have given me a gift with more meaning."

Phillip looked a little embarrassed. "It was a little different from what I'd planned."

Rafaelo sank back down on the sofa beside Caitlyn and

reached for her hand. Heath, Megan and Joshua all looked expectant.

"What are you giving Rafaelo?" asked Alyssa, leaning over Joshua's shoulder.

"Hush," said Megan. "It's a surprise."

Even Amy looked interested.

Phillip waited. Once everyone had fallen silent, he said with great ceremony, "As a thank-you for rescuing Caitlyn and all the Saxon horses I'd like to give you that Devil Horse."

Rafaelo felt overwhelmed. "Thank you. I will value him every day."

"It's your job to get him to Spain," Phillip said gruffly, as Rafaelo clasped his arm.

"But that's not what we—"

"Hush, Megan, you'll give it away."

Phillip gave a slow smile. "My children are impatient. Come," he summoned them all around him. They crowded around the sofa where Rafaelo and Caitlyn sat. Joshua stood at his right shoulder, Megan on his left and Heath a little out of the fold at the back. Rafaelo was painfully aware of Kay's absence. Meeting Phillip's eyes, he read pain and regret. Phillip was missing his wife. Rafaelo's hand tightened around Caitlyn's.

"We have talked. We have reached an agreement—all of us, even Heath." Phillip paused, then added, "Even Kay. Rafaelo, I would like to give you a share equal to my other children in Saxon's Folly."

Rafaelo went rigid.

Caitlyn grew still beside him.

No words would come. Rafaelo cleared his throat, the emotion of the moment surrounding him. He rose to his feet and stepped forward.

"Kay agreed to this?"

Phillip nodded. "I spoke to her about it—she feels you are entitled to your share of Saxon's Folly."

Rafaelo could see that the conversation had not been easy. Phillip had a lot to make up for. But perhaps by calling Kay, Phillip had taken the first step.

"I can never tell you how much this means to me." Rafaelo met Joshua's gaze, then Heath's. Black eyes. So like his.

Megan wasn't as restrained. She flung her arms around him. "It's great having another brother, especially such a cute one."

He laughed. He was aware of Caitlyn grinning from the comfort of the sofa—laughing at him, damn it. But he knew that she trusted him. Trusted him not to sell the stake he'd just been given. As he'd threatened to do what seemed like a lifetime ago.

Phillip cleared his throat. "Rafaelo, son, I owe you an apology. I've already apologised to Maria."

"Thank you." His mother had told him—and that meant the world to him.

Now he waited.

"I'm sorry that I never took responsibility for you, for thinking that paying Maria a good sum for the journals absolved me of my paternal responsibilities." Phillip sighed. "Hell, I didn't even know she was pregnant when I made that offer, but I justified it in my mind. I did try to trace her later to offer her a lump sum for your upbringing. But she had vanished."

His mother had become Marquesa de Las Carreras. She hadn't needed Phillip's money, she never had. She'd wanted his love. But that had been impossible.

He glanced at Caitlyn. He'd come here talking grandly of honour. But she'd made him a better man. If it hadn't been for her, he doubted he would ever have realised the significance of his journey to Hawkes Bay. For the first time he acknowledged that he'd travelled across the world in the unspoken hope that his father would apologise for the decades of neglect.

What he hadn't expected was to be able to forgive him, to forge a bond that would last with his blood father, his brothers…and his father's wife. He suspected this was what his papa's final legacy to him had been: a family.

"Thank you for the offer. I appreciate it more than I can ever say but—"

He glanced again at Caitlyn. She still smiled. He knew without doubt that the desire for vengeance had gone forever…replaced by desire of another kind.

For them love was possible.

He took a deep breath. "But I can't accept it."

There was dead silence. Phillip's face fell, Megan's mouth dropped open and even Joshua looked disconcerted.

"But my lawyer—"

"My lawyer has instructions to contact him to say that the negotiations are over. I no longer hunger for a share in Saxon's Folly or for revenge." Rafaelo started to smile. "But there is something else I would like to take back with me. Something infinitely more valuable than a share in Saxon's Folly."

"What could be more valuable?" Typically, it was Megan who asked.

"Your winemaker."

Megan laughed. "You're that keen on our sherry?"

Caitlyn looked apprehensive. She shook her head at him. But Rafaelo was not about to stop. He'd screwed this up before, he wasn't going to screw it up again.

He bent down on one knee in front of Caitlyn, he picked up her hand and was aware that the salon had gone utterly still. "Will you do me the honour of marrying me?"

Her mouth barely moved, but he saw the word shaped on her lips. *Why?*

"Not because you are beautiful and sexy." Behind him he heard Megan whoop. "Not because I enjoy listening to everything you say." Alyssa started to laugh. "Not because I'm trying to get an inside track on the best *finos* sherry in the world." This time Phillip growled and Heath laughed beside him. "Not because I want you more than any woman I have ever met."

"Rafaelo!" Caitlyn flushed scarlet. But her eyes glowed. "Be sensible."

"I'm not interested in sensible. I know that I am asking you to take a big step, to come with me back to Spain. The only reason I can justify asking you to marry me is because I love you."

He fell silent. And waited. The rest of the room faded away. He was aware of only Caitlyn's clear crystal eyes and the tenderness in his heart.

"You love me?" There was amazement…and something more.

She had told him she would only marry for love. He would honour that.

"I do." It was in the nature of a vow. And he knew he would never let her forget it.

"Then the answer must be yes."

This time it was Rafaelo who whooped. He straightened to his full height, swung her up into his arms, twirled her around and brought his lips down on hers.

When they came up for air, he was as breathless as she.

"I think we need a little air," Caitlyn managed, pulling him toward the French doors. "We'll be back in a while," she threw over her shoulder, as she led him out into the starry night.

Outside she turned into his arms. "I love you, too."

"I suspected," he said with a touch of the arrogance that was ingrained.

"You did, did you?"

"Of course. Otherwise you would never have let me kiss you…touch you. You loved me."

* * *

Back at the Vintner's Cottage, it was late. Caitlyn lay sprawled across Rafaelo's chest, her face flushed with kisses. Happiness warmed her like summer sunshine.

"Thank you for giving me so many priceless treasures," he murmured, lifting his head from where he'd been nibbling at her neck.

She lifted her eyelids, and gave him a lazy stare. "Which treasures are you thinking about?"

"A new family—complete with brothers and sisters. Your love." He kissed the tip of her nose. "Yourself."

She made a moaning sound of utter delight.

"Are you sure you can bring yourself to leave Saxon's Folly?" he asked softly, a tinge of concern shadowing the joy in his eyes.

"My home is where you are, Rafaelo," she said. "And if that means living in the midst of the Jerez triangle, overlooking the Atlantic and producing *finos* sherry, then that sounds pretty damn wonderful."

"I was thinking about that," said Rafaelo. "We can visit Saxon's Folly often. And there's no reason why Saxon's Folly can't import sherry from Torres Carreras—and sell real, honest sherry."

"That's a wonderful idea. We can discuss it with Megan and Phillip tomorrow." Caitlyn drew back to stare into his eyes. "I can't wait to see Torres Carreras, to meet your mother."

"You'll love it there. My mother can't wait to meet you either. I spent most of my time on the phone to her earlier telling her how fabulous you are, how much I hoped you would agree to marry me."

"You weren't sure?"

He looked sheepish. "No. In one corner of my heart I didn't know whether you would be able to bring yourself to leave the Saxons—and Saxon's Folly."

"I feel bad about leaving them without a winemaker. But

Heath lives just over The Divide and he's more than capable of bringing in two harvests a year."

A thoughtful expression crossed his face. "I might have a word with him."

She laughed. "I can't believe you two are talking."

"I think we've sorted out our differences," he said with a touch of smugness.

"You know, I think I've been very silly."

"Why?"

"I rather suspect that thinking I was in love with Heath was a big smokescreen so that I didn't need to worry about guys. About dating anyone."

"Nothing silly about that. Sounds smart to me."

She drew a line along his lower lip. "I will tell you I never experienced anything like this dizzying desire for Heath even though I told myself I was in love with him for years."

"And that is why the man is still alive."

"Rafaelo! You're a brute."

"You're mine," he said, pulling her close, plastering her up against him and claiming her with a kiss so passionate that her legs gave out.

Or had she merely been in love with the idea of being in love? Trapped in her studies, had Heath been nothing more than a safe guy to fancy? And after the horrific incident with Tommy, she'd had no desire for romance and her crush on Heath had simply become a habit—a knee-jerk reaction.

It didn't matter anymore.

Rafaelo was the real deal.

She reached up and pressed a kiss on his lips. He tasted delicious. Then planted another kiss on the scar below his lip. "Hmm. I've been wanting to do that for a long time. Tell me how you got that."

His lips twitched. "I fell off my bicycle when I was five years old. One of the handlebars pierced my flesh."

"Ouch." Caitlyn pulled a face. "And there I thought it was from bullfighting. Or street fighting." She clicked her tongue.

"Oh, I have those scars, too." His eyes glittered with wickedness. "Do you want to see them?"

"You're having me on," she said uncertainly.

He gave her an indecipherable look. "Wanna bet?"

"No! Bad idea," she said firmly. "I have no intention of losing to you ever again."

And she kissed him again.

A fair time later, Caitlyn raised her head. "Do you really have scars?"

He nodded. "At least one really impressive one where a bull gored me when I was young and foolish."

Horror shook her. Then curiosity set in. "Can I see it? Touch it?"

He groaned something that sounded like "witch." And it was a long time before either of them spoke or laughed—or took on a bet.

* * * * *

Don't miss the next book in
THE SAXON BRIDES *series,*
PREGNANCY PROPOSAL,
available in December
from Silhouette Desire.

Tanner heard the rig roll in around sunset. Smiling, he wandered to the window. Watched as Olivia O'Ballivan climbed out of her Suburban, flung one defiant glance toward the house and started for the barn, the golden retriever trotting along behind her.

Taking his coat and hat down from the peg next to the back door, he put them on and went outside. He was used to being alone, even liked it, but keeping company with Doc O'Ballivan, bristly though she sometimes was, would provide a welcome diversion.

He gave her time to reach the horse Butterpie's stall, then walked into the barn.

The golden retriever came to greet him, all wagging tail and melting brown eyes, and he bent to stroke her soft, sturdy back. "Hey, there, dog," he said.

Sure enough, Olivia was in the stall, brushing Butterpie down and talking to her in a soft, soothing voice that touched something private inside Tanner and made him want to turn on one heel and beat it back to the house.

He'd be damned if he'd do it, though.

This was *his* ranch, *his* barn. Well-intentioned as she was, *Olivia* was the trespasser here, not him.

"She's still very upset," Olivia told him, without turning to look at him or slowing down with the brush.

Shiloh, always an easy horse to get along with, stood contentedly in his own stall, munching away on the feed Tanner had given him earlier. Butterpie, he noted, hadn't touched her supper as far as he could tell.

"Do you know anything at all about horses, Mr. Quinn?" Olivia asked.

He leaned against the stall door, the way he had the day before, and grinned. He'd practically been raised on horseback; he and Tessa had grown up on their grandmother's farm in the Texas Hill Country, after their folks divorced and went their separate ways, both of them too busy to bother with a couple of kids. "A few things," he said. "And I mean to call you Olivia, so you might as well return the favor and address me by my first name."

He watched as she took that in, dealt with it, decided on an approach. He'd have to wait and see what that turned out to be, but he didn't mind. It was a pleasure just watching Olivia O'Ballivan grooming a horse.

"All right, *Tanner*," she said. "This barn is a disgrace. When are you going to have the roof fixed? If it snows again, the hay will get wet and probably mold…."

He chuckled, shifted a little. He'd have a crew out there the following Monday morning to replace the roof and shore up the walls—he'd made the arrangements over a week before—but he felt no particular compunction to explain that. He was enjoying her ire too much; it made her colour rise and her hair fly when she turned her head, and the faster breathing made her perfect breasts go up and down in an enticing rhythm. "What makes you so sure I'm a greenhorn?" he asked mildly, still leaning on the gate.

At last she looked straight at him, but she didn't move from Butterpie's side. "Your hat, your boots—that fancy red truck you drive. I'll bet it's customized."

Tanner grinned. Adjusted his hat. "Are you telling me real cowboys don't drive red trucks?"

"There are lots of trucks around here," she said. "Some of them are red, and some of them are new. And *all* of them are splattered with mud or manure or both."

"Maybe I ought to put in a car wash, then," he teased. "Sounds like there's a market for one. Might be a good investment."

She softened, though not significantly, and spared him a cautious half smile, full of questions she probably wouldn't ask. "There's a good car wash in Indian Rock," she informed him. "People go there. It's only forty miles."

"Oh," he said with just a hint of mockery. "*Only* forty miles. Well, then. Guess I'd better dirty up my truck if I want to be taken seriously in these here parts. Scuff up my boots a bit, too, and maybe stomp on my hat a couple of times."

Her cheeks went a fetching shade of pink. "You are twisting what I said," she told him, brushing Butterpie again, her touch gentle but sure. "I meant…"

Tanner envied that little horse. Wished he had a furry hide, so he'd need brushing, too.

"You *meant* that I'm not a real cowboy," he said. "And you could be right. I've spent a lot of time on construction sites over the last few years, or in meetings where a hat and boots wouldn't be appropriate. Instead of digging out my old gear, once I decided to take this job, I just bought new."

"I bet you don't even *have* any old gear," she challenged, but she was smiling, albeit cautiously, as though she might withdraw into a disapproving frown at any second.

He took off his hat, extended it to her. "Here," he teased. "Rub that around in the muck until it suits you."

She laughed, and the sound—well, it caused a powerful and wholly unexpected shift inside him. Scared the hell out of him and, paradoxically, made him yearn to hear it again.

* * * * *

*Discover how this rugged rancher's wanderlust
is tamed in time for a merry Christmas, in
A STONE CREEK CHRISTMAS.
In stores December 2008.*

Silhouette®

SPECIAL EDITION™

FROM *NEW YORK TIMES* BESTSELLING AUTHOR

LINDA LAEL MILLER

A STONE CREEK CHRISTMAS

Veterinarian Olivia O'Ballivan finds the animals in Stone Creek playing Cupid between her and Tanner Quinn. Even Tanner's daughter, Sophie, is eager to play matchmaker. With everyone conspiring against them and the holiday season fast approaching, Tanner and Olivia may just get everything they want for Christmas after all!

*Available December 2008
wherever books are sold.*

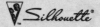

SPECIAL EDITION™

MISTLETOE AND MIRACLES

by *USA TODAY* bestselling author

MARIE FERRARELLA

Child psychologist Trent Marlowe couldn't believe his eyes when Laurel Greer, the woman he'd loved and lost, came to him for help. Now a widow, with a troubled boy who wouldn't speak, Laurel needed a miracle from Trent…and a brief detour under the mistletoe wouldn't hurt, either.

Available in December wherever books are sold.

EXTRA

THE ITALIAN'S BRIDE
Commanded—to be his wife!

Used to the finest food, clothes and women,
these immensely powerful, incredibly
good-looking and undeniably charismatic
men have only one last need: a wife!

They've chosen their bride-to-be and they'll
have her—willing or not!

Enjoy all our fantastic stories in December:

THE ITALIAN BILLIONAIRE'S
SECRET LOVE-CHILD
by CATHY WILLIAMS (Book #33)

SICILIAN MILLIONAIRE,
BOUGHT BRIDE
by CATHERINE SPENCER (Book #34)

BEDDED AND WEDDED FOR REVENGE
by MELANIE MILBURNE (Book #35)

THE ITALIAN'S UNWILLING WIFE
by KATHRYN ROSS (Book #36)

REQUEST YOUR FREE BOOKS!

2 FREE NOVELS PLUS 2 FREE GIFTS!

Silhouette®

Desire®

Passionate, Powerful, Provocative!

YES! Please send me 2 FREE Silhouette Desire® novels and my 2 FREE gifts (gifts are worth about $10). After receiving them, if I don't wish to receive any more books, I can return the shipping statement marked "cancel." If I don't cancel, I will receive 6 brand-new novels every month and be billed just $4.05 per book in the U.S. or $4.74 per book in Canada, plus 25¢ shipping and handling per book and applicable taxes, if any*. That's a savings of almost 15% off the cover price! I understand that accepting the 2 free books and gifts places me under no obligation to buy anything. I can always return a shipment and cancel at any time. Even if I never buy another book, the two free books and gifts are mine to keep forever.

225 SDN ERVX 326 SDN ERVM

Name	(PLEASE PRINT)

Address	Apt. #

City	State/Prov.	Zip/Postal Code

Signature (if under 18, a parent or guardian must sign)

Mail to the Silhouette Reader Service:
IN U.S.A.: P.O. Box 1867, Buffalo, NY 14240-1867
IN CANADA: P.O. Box 609, Fort Erie, Ontario L2A 5X3

Not valid to current subscribers of Silhouette Desire books.

Want to try two free books from another line?
Call 1-800-873-8635 or visit www.morefreebooks.com.

* Terms and prices subject to change without notice. N.Y. residents add applicable sales tax. Canadian residents will be charged applicable provincial taxes and GST. Offer not valid in Quebec. This offer is limited to one order per household. All orders subject to approval. Credit or debit balances in a customer's account(s) may be offset by any other outstanding balance owed by or to the customer. Please allow 4 to 6 weeks for delivery. Offer available while quantities last.

Your Privacy: Silhouette Books is committed to protecting your privacy. Our Privacy Policy is available online at www.eHarlequin.com or upon request from the Reader Service. From time to time we make our lists of customers available to reputable third parties who may have a product or service of interest to you. If you would prefer we not share your name and address, please check here. ☐

SDES08R